To Wendy!

Best Wishes

Carol M Creasey

2022

C000227553

PERFECTLY EVIL

Also by Carol M. Creasey:

Biography:
My Life is Worth Living!
Candidly Carol

Fiction:
Fatal Obsession
Not Just an Affair
Evil Woman
Evil Woman...Takes Revenge
The Power of Love
One Moment of Madness
Nobody's Perfect
Please Forgive Me!

Perfectly Evil

A Murder Mystery

Carol M. Creasey

UNITED WRITERS
Cornwall

UNITED WRITERS PUBLICATIONS LTD
Ailsa, Castle Gate, Penzance, Cornwall.
www.unitedwriters.co.uk

British Library Cataloguing in Publication Data:
A catalogue record for this book is
available from the British Library.

ISBN 9781852002015

Printed and bound in Great Britain by
United Writers Publications Ltd.,
Cornwall.

I dedicate this book to my dear friends
Lesley and Jon, who helped me
through difficult times.
God bless you! xx

Chapter One

"Dee, you are not going anywhere until you do your homework!"

Lydia's voice had a trace of desperation in it, but her tone was firm. She felt she had every right to be strict about this. The private school that her stepdaughter attended charged very high fees, so it was up to her and Nathan to make sure she did her homework to justify the cost.

How she wished that Nathan was at home; he was better at dealing with his hormonal sixteen-year-old daughter. Even though he wasn't her biological father, he had been a part of her life ever since she had been just a few months old, whereas Lydia had been her stepmother for the past ten years.

Lydia had been very happy to do this, having already spent a year working for the Morton Brown family as a Nanny for Dee ever since her mother had been tragically killed in a road accident. Working for the family and supporting Nathan in his grief had felt right; she, too, had been recovering from a traumatic situation. After losing a pregnancy, and leaving a violent husband, she found working for the Morton Brown family actually helped her with her own grief.

When she found out how Dee, who had actually been christened Danielle but now preferred to have her name shortened to Dee, had been reunited with her mother at four years old, and then had tragically witnessed the suicide of her unbalanced Nanny Alice, not long before her own mother's death, she realised that winning Dee's trust was not going to be easy.

Her concerned grandfather, Philip Morton Brown, had arranged grief counselling for Dee. Maria Firth, from Harley Street, came to the house, as they felt it would be better for Dee to be in familiar surroundings. Philip and Isabel had explained that happy-go-lucky and easy tempered Dee had changed her personality since her mother died, and had become withdrawn and depressed. So as a family they had to break down those barriers, and make the little girl feel as if her life had meaning again. Apparently, she had adored her mother; and now, at the age of sixteen, she looked just like her, with dark hair and very brown eyes, a real beauty with perfect cheekbones.

Lydia had been told by Nathan that their looks had been where the similarity ended. Sadie's personality had been dark and mysterious, whereas Dee was uncomplicated, with a ready smile and a sense of fun. Her eyes sparkled with warmth, and she was a happy little girl.

It had taken Lydia, with the help of the family, and Maria, a year to get Dee to trust her, but when she saw her happy-go-lucky nature emerging, it was so rewarding, and she then shared many hugs with her, as Dee was spontaneously affectionate.

Being united in grief had made her become close to Nathan. He felt like a knight in shining armour who had come along and rescued her; just by being himself and making her realise that there were some decent men in the world, and not everyone had a violent temper like her soon to be ex-husband had.

When her divorce came through, she had by then already realised that she was falling in love with Nathan, but said nothing until the day he admitted he was in love with her . Philip and Isabel were so happy that he had found love again, and she felt like she had been given another chance of happiness. When they got married, it was like a dream come true, her handsome husband was the complete opposite of the first one, being gentle, patient and loving. She had been delighted to become Dee's step mother.

Her miscarriage had caused internal damage, and she had been told by doctors that she might never conceive again. Unfortunately, the doctors had been proved to be right, and because both her and Nathan wanted Dee to grow up with a sibling, two years after IVF treatment had failed, they adopted Jack. He was nine years old at the time, and his mother had been Lydia's closest friend. She had brought him up on her own because as soon as she told his father she was pregnant he had left her. Jack's mother was only thirty-two, but she had died from a brain tumour, and Lydia didn't like the idea of this nine-year-old boy going into care, and neither did Nathan. She felt it was the only thing left that she could do for Emily, so they had willingly offered Jack a home with them.

All these thoughts were running through her head as she saw the mutinous expression on Dee's face, with her hand poised on the door handle. She was dressed in hot pants, with a low top that would have caused her father to insist she went back upstairs and change. Her very dark hair was tied up into a ponytail, which made her look younger than her sixteen years, her shapely legs were tanned due to living on the Kent coast, and she had quite a lot of make-up on, which she didn't really need because she was a natural beauty. Her lipstick was bright red, and her eyes were heavily and dramatically made up, but to try telling that to a teenager; it was a waste of time. She was a child trying so hard to be an adult, and yet she had all the time in the world ahead of her. As their eyes met, Dee paused, then turned from the door dramatically:

"You don't tell me what to do. You are not my mother!" and with that she burst into tears and ran up the stairs towards her room, and then Lydia heard her bedroom door bang shut.

Lydia felt the pain of rejection flood through her, and she wondered where they had gone wrong. For the last two years Dee had turned into a person that neither of them recognised. She had become moody, withdrawn and rebellious. She had always got good reports from her first school, so they felt she had earned her place at a private school, and hopefully it would give her the best chance in life. Nathan had a good and very well paid job; he had really made something of himself, and he wanted Dee to have the best opportunities in life. For three years she had been a model pupil; she made new friends and worked hard, and was popular with the teachers.

But at fourteen it was noticeable how much she changed, and ever since then it had been hard work to understand her. Jack was not the problem; they got on fine together, so it wasn't jealousy. And at school, for some reason, she had lost her popularity, except with Beth who was her closest friend. Beth was as blonde as Dee was dark. She was a very pretty girl with a ready smile, and earnest innocent looking big blue eyes. She was very loyal to Dee. Even when Dee was being withdrawn, Beth seemed to understand her. Both Lydia and Nathan had told Dee many times how lucky she was to have someone who stuck by her through thick and thin.

They had even visited the school and spoken to her teachers to try and find out what the problem was, but they were not forthcoming either, so it was hoped Dee was just being a teenager and would grow out of this difficult phase.

At that moment the door opened to admit Jack, he was the same age as Dee but taller and gangly. He had brown hair and eyes, and wore glasses. After living with them for seven years, he was well and truly established as one of the family. But he called them Nathan and Lydia, which was understandable, as having lived with his mother for nine years before she died, he could still remember her well.

Jack was a quiet and studious lad; he enjoyed maths and sciences, and had done very well at school. He had never given them any cause for concern, and was shortly due to take his GCSEs. His only fault was, like most teenagers, he spent more time than he should either on his laptop or playing computer games. Nathan had tried to encourage him to play football and do more sports, but Jack knew what he liked. He rode his bike more or less everywhere he went, and went swimming at the pool in Herne Bay.

Today was a warm day in early May, and when Jack removed his protective helmet, he was sweating underneath. Lydia guessed he had been cycling quite fast to get home.

"Hi Lydia, I could murder a cold drink," he said cheerily.

"Of course, lots of cans in the fridge. How was school today?"

"It was fine. Less than two weeks until our exams now."

"You won't have any problems," said Lydia encouragingly, and she knew he would be fine. But she couldn't help worrying about Dee. All schools started their GCSE exams in the middle of May, but what about Dee? She was throwing her life away, not seemingly interested in doing well in her exams, and they had no idea why.

"Dee's in her room, I had to stop her going out."

Jack pulled a face. "Oh dear, she won't like that. Maybe I should pop in her room and cheer her up."

"Would you, Jack? You can make her laugh."

This is what Lydia and Nathan both liked about Jack. Behind his glasses and scholastic appearance was another side to him. He had a droll sense of humour, and Dee really looked up to him. She was less dramatic when he was around, and they were as close as if they were blood siblings.

She watched as he grabbed two cans of diet coke from the fridge, then he gave her a wink and headed upstairs as fast as his long gangly legs would allow him to move. A wave of affection coursed through her. He was past the age of hugging, but Jack had a way of defusing a situation, and she was so glad they had given him a home. To her Dee and Jack felt like they were her children. Even though she had not given birth to them, it was the everyday life they all shared together that created the bonds between them.

Jack grinned to himself when he heard the loud music pulsating from Dee's room. That meant she was angry, but it was a harmless way of letting off steam, better than screaming obscenities at one another; that wasn't Dee's style, she knew better than to swear at home. What people might have considered 'bad language' years ago was now thought of as nothing. When teenagers expressed bad feelings between themselves, no one took any notice, but one place it wasn't acceptable was around the house, as adults didn't have the same tolerance towards it. He knew he had a way of disarming Dee; although she was by nature a quiet girl, she had a feisty side to her too. He thought of her as his little sister, partly because she was a lot shorter than him, and also she was a few months younger, although they were in the same year at school.

He had to bang on the door or else she wouldn't have heard him, and her reply was exactly as he expected:

"Go away!"

"Dee, it's me, I've got a can of coke out here for you."

Dee opened the door slowly; her face was flushed. He held the can out to her, so she opened the door even wider and he went inside. Her room was always immaculately tidy, unlike his; his bed was covered in clothes and unmade, but hers was neatly made, with the pillows fluffed up and cushions at the head of it. He perched at the foot of it.

"She won't let me go out!"

"Lydia, you mean? Where do you want to go?"

"It's just a film at the Kavanagh Cinema; a comedy. We fancied a final bit of fun before our exams started."

"Lydia actually said you couldn't go?"

Dee coloured, knowing that was not strictly true. "She said not until I had done my homework. But it's Friday, I could do it tomorrow."

"You could, but I think Philip and Isabel are coming round tomorrow. Billy is over again. Lydia probably hoped you would do some last minute revising, to make yourself free for when our grandparents, and your other brother, came to tea."

Dee had always trusted Jack as much as she trusted Beth, but she still couldn't bring herself to share the secret that was causing so much turmoil inside her. She knew it made her behave irrationally towards those she loved. She had only confided in Beth, and she was trying to give her some support with it, but she didn't feel that she could share this with her parents, especially Nathan. She could still remember just how much he had loved her mother, as she had too. In fact, she had idolised her mother, and had been so proud of the fact that people commented about how much she looked like her.

She could never forget the day that Nathan had told her that her mother had been killed in a road accident, it was etched on her mind forever. He hadn't been able to hold back the tears, and they had wept together. It was the same with her grandparents. Philip and Isabel were also consumed with grief. It was a grief that united them even more, and it was a grief that Billy could never share with them because he had never known his mother, and so had no memories of her. Maybe if Sadie were here now, Billy might not be part of the family, as until she had died, Billy's existence had not been known about. His father Ricky just happened to be visiting England when the accident occurred, and, of course, came to her funeral. That was another day that Dee would never forget; sitting with Nathan and her grandparents behind the hearse that carried her beloved mother's body. It had somehow seemed unreal.

12

Discovering she had a half-brother had in no way diminished her grief at losing her mother. He had been brought up in America, and they just weren't that close, although she had nothing against him.

With the help of Lydia and Maria, they had worked through their grief, and when Nathan married Lydia, she had felt safe and loved again. Three years after that Jack became part of their family, and even though there were no blood ties, he felt like a brother, more than Billy ever had, and she loved the fact that he lived with them. Both Dee and Jack had lost their mothers in tragic circumstances, long before their time should have been due, so they were both aware of the pain that caused. In the case of Dee, she realised how much it had helped them all by having Lydia in their lives. When Nathan married her, it made Dee feel more secure. She loved her, of course, but she loved the memory of her mother more, and would always regret her tragic loss.

As for Jack, he had only ever known his mother. She had brought him up alone, which had made them incredibly close. Lydia had been around and a part of his life ever since he could remember, being his mother's closest friend. So coming to live with Lydia and Nathan was the best possible outcome of an incredibly sad situation. He liked and respected Nathan, he was like the father he had never known, and he also had the added bonus of more grandparents, as his mother's parents lived in New Zealand, so most of the contact with them was through Skype. He had never felt close to them because they had wanted his mother to abort him. As her partner had left her, they were more concerned about the fact that their daughter would be an unmarried mother, than the joy of having a healthy grandson. But after her death they realised how petty that had been, and offered him a home in New Zealand. Jack didn't know them, and he opted to stay in England with Lydia and Nathan. Philip and Isabel seemed delighted to have him as part of their family, so he knew he had made the right choice.

He couldn't fail to notice that Dee was having problems. When he had first moved in with them all she was doing so well at school. Then she had passed the entrance exam to St Martha's with ease, and up until about two years ago, she had been top of her class in most subjects. He had wondered if she had a secret boyfriend who was distracting her from her school work, or was she distracted because she was struggling towards maturity with hidden ghosts inside her mind which were left over from her past?

Today she had obviously tangled with Lydia, who only had her best intentions at heart, and surely Dee must know this. He wondered if he should step in and try to persuade Lydia to let her go to the cinema, but then he abandoned the idea. Lydia had made a stand and it would cause trouble if he interfered, especially if Dee failed her exams. He could imagine that going to the cinema with Beth was important to Dee, as it seemed like she had dumped her other friends. No one called for her to go out any more. Jenny, round the corner, used to. He knew Dee had even committed the cardinal sin of deleting her Facebook page. With the way she was feeling now, this wasn't the best time to question it.

"Well sis, the film is still on next week. Would you like me to test you on anything?"

Dee shook her head. She wished she could explain to him how important it was for her to be seen with Beth at the cinema. There was no way she could tell anyone why she had no longer had any other friends at school. Nor could she explain the abuse she had received on social media from persons unknown. This was why she had come off Facebook. It was all raging around inside her, threatening to erupt and drive her crazy. She was determined to go to the cinema tonight, if it was the last thing she ever did.

"Jack, you are great you know. I will be OK. Now go and play your computer games, I know you want to. I am going to lock my door and get on with revising without being disturbed."

"If you are sure?" Jack couldn't wait to open up his PC; he was self-disciplined enough to do some revising as well. He didn't feel he could do any more to help Dee. She was going to revise, it seemed. He knew how keen she was to get into the sixth form, so it had to be done.

She smiled at him, her anger now forgotten. "Yes, I am sure, and thanks for the coke."

Dee opened the door to let him out, and then closed it and locked it again. The next thing was to text Beth and say she was leaving soon. After doing that, she turned her music off; there was always a chance that Lydia might come up and ask her to anyway, and if it was all silent they would assume she was revising.

She checked that her hair looked OK, and then wiped the tears of frustration off her face with a tissue. Her make-up needed to be repaired. She reapplied some lipstick and renewed her eye make-up.

Maybe it was a bit of a drastic way to get out, but at this end of the house, if she could get downstairs quietly, Lydia would be up the other end in the kitchen or the lounge, and she could escape through the conservatory.

She cautiously opened the bedroom door, then locked it again and pocketed the key. Jack had now gone to his room, so she crept down the stairs. She could hear Lydia moving about in the kitchen. She went along the passage the other way, and, as she had expected, the conservatory was empty. The door creaked a little as she opened it, and she held her breath. The key was in the lock, so she locked it again, and pocketed that key as well. That would be her way back later. Then she ran down the path to the gate on tiptoe, only stopping to walk at a normal rate after she had closed the gate behind her.

This was the only way to exit the house on foot, as the gravel outside the kitchen window made a noise when anyone walked upon it, and there was also a long drive to negotiate before arriving at the iron security gates. That entrance was only used by anyone arriving or departing in a car. Now that she felt free, she hurried down the hill towards the cinema to meet Beth.

Nathan felt anxious when he got the text from Lydia. Dee was playing up again, and they couldn't work out why. The way she was going it was unlikely she would pass her exams, and it was such a shame as she was a bright girl. But to him the most important thing was her happiness; she had faced so much tragedy in her short life, but he thought they had coped with that, they had all had to rebuild their lives. Now Dee seemed to have gone downhill again. If only he could find out why.

He couldn't allow her to grow up out of control because of the tragedy they had suffered, it was not an excuse for bad behaviour. And poor Lydia had been like a mother to her these past ten years, without expecting to be recognised as such. It was not on for Dee to speak to her like that. He would definitely have words with her about it!

He decided to leave for home now, it was already four thirty, and the traffic in Canterbury was building up. The journey to Herne Bay was only a few miles, but right now the roads would be full of cars with parents bringing their children home from school.

He drove past the house he had shared very briefly with Sadie and Dee some ten years ago. Why was it, even now, whenever he passed it he remembered that black box with Sadie's diary in, and the revelations it had contained? That was a secret that only Nathan and Lydia shared, and sometimes the weight of it filled him with guilt. But for the sake of Philip and Isabel, as well as Dee, it was a secret that had to be kept.

Nathan hadn't been able to face living in the house at Canterbury after Sadie's tragic accident, so he had brought Dee back to Herne Bay, and they stayed with Philip and Isabel in their beautiful period house on the downs. Sadie had been instrumental in helping her mother to recover from cancer. She had taken her for treatment, and helped her to regain her confidence, and Isabel had kept that memory inside her. It comforted her that after losing Sadie her last memory was a happy one, so there was no way Nathan would ever spoil that.

Philip and Isabel had decided, when Nathan married Lydia, that they wanted to move to a bungalow, as there were only two of them, and they wanted Nathan and the family to stay on in the house. So Nathan decided they were not just going to have any bungalow. He bought a piece of land at Reculver, and they were able to plan their dream home overlooking Reculver Towers and the rugged coastline that stretched along to Thanet.

Nathan had employed an army of workers to build it quickly, and when the time came for them to move in, it stood resplendent, with panoramic views across the North Sea. They now lived fairly close to one another without being right on top of one another. By car the journey took about ten minutes.

He had kept Dee's behaviour problems from Philip and Isabel, as he had hoped she would grow out of it. They were getting on in years now, and had already faced many tragedies after losing both their son when he was very young, and then their daughter. It was no wonder that Nathan and Lydia, with their family of Dee and Jack, meant so much to them

As he drove up the winding drive of his house, with trees on either side, he decided he was going to have a chat with Dee, and try to restore harmony in the house. They had already had enough drama in their lives to last a lifetime.

Chapter Two

Janet Philpott hated her name, and just about everything about herself, particularly the spots which persisted in covering her face in spite of all the creams she used to rid herself of them. The doctor had told her she would grow out of them. But she wondered how that could be, not understanding that her age and her spots had any connection.

She also hated her boring brown hair, it hung lank and straight, but she had been able to do something about that. She had coloured it with a reddish brown tone, which not only gave her face some warmth, but also improved the condition of her hair. Janet also used foundation to cover her spots, but she felt that under this attractive exterior she was still plain Janet Philpott.

Her parents both had high flying careers. Her father was a prominent barrister, and her mother ran a modelling agency ever since her own very successful career had come to an end. Neither of them had much spare time to spend with Janet, so it was no wonder she had no self-esteem. She had been at St Martha's School with Dee and Beth for the past two years.

Janet was only too aware of just how spiteful and bitchy teenage girls could be to one another. She had experienced it herself at her last school in London, so she knew what it was like to be an outsider. The fact that St Martha's was an exclusive private school made no difference. Who could know whether the teachers were aware of the bullying that went on? Because if they did, then they chose to turn a blind eye to it.

So Janet made a decision, when she joined the new school, that she was not going to be a victim any more. She became immediately aware of a secret gang called St Martha's Girls; they were controlled by a mobile phone belonging to 'the boss'. She was going to make sure she kept in with the one who had the power. The rights and wrongs of the situation didn't come into it. Not knowing exactly who 'the boss' was made the situation all the more scary, but the person was definitely someone she would never cross.

Janet knew what her duty was; it was to intimidate Dee, then drive all her friends away. She had certainly achieved that, as Dee only had her loyal friend Beth left now. It had been very easy to upset her, personal insults rolled off her back, but bringing up her mother's infamous past had really riled her. How on earth 'the boss' had all this information was something Janet couldn't fathom out. It had been years ago, if it was even true. Apparently Dee's mother Sadie had been accused of murdering her lover, a well known footballer called Danny Foster, some fourteen years ago. It had never been proved, as she had been deemed unfit to stand trial and then shut away in a funny farm for four years.

Janet played her part well, taunting Dee for having a mother who was mad and dangerous, and she even suggested that maybe Dee had taken after her. Dee fought back; she wasn't having anyone spoiling her mother's memory, and she defended her mother to the hilt. Her memories had been of a kind, compassionate woman who always had time for her. They had enjoyed karaoke evenings together, as Sadie had a really good singing voice, and every evening at bedtime her mother had read stories to her.

But gradually all her friends had left her except Beth. Nobody wanted to be involved with her, and then an unknown person had posted vile and abusive messages on her Facebook page, so she had no choice but to delete it. Dee was the only girl in her class without a Facebook page.

Janet felt that being vile to Dee was the only way she would stop herself from being a victim. She didn't particularly hate her, she didn't really hate anyone, but she never forgot the bullying she had received at her previous school in London, and how bad it had made her feel. Any guilt she had about it had been firmly squashed down.

19

The irony of the situation was that Janet was having an on and off affair with Dee's half-brother Billy, every time he jetted into England from his home in New York. She had never told Billy what she was doing, as he might not like the idea that she was bullying his half-sister, whether they were close or not. She had found out that at this school it was dog eat dog, so it was her way of looking after herself, rather than the right way, which would have been to tell her parents exactly what was going on, and helping to expose 'the boss', who had such a hold over her.

She knew she was far from perfect, but even Billy had a chip on his shoulder, as he shared the same mother as Dee, being Sadie's son by her first marriage to Ricky Scott. By all accounts, after the marriage had ended, Billy had been put up for adoption by Sadie, and Simon and Jill Hopkins had been the ones to bring him up.

He had grown up in very poor surroundings, so when he found out that he had rich relatives in England, he couldn't wait to meet them. He had boasted to Janet that Philip and Isabel had welcomed him into the family, and invited him to stay at their luxury home. He now popped backwards and forwards across the Atlantic Ocean as often as he could, and he was hoping to continue his studies in England. At the age of twenty he knew he wanted a comfortable lifestyle, so maybe staying with his grandparents would achieve that.

She knew he wasn't that close to Dee, having not grown up with her, so they shared nothing more than a polite relationship. He had found Dee rather quiet, so had made no attempt to get on her wavelength. Janet had been careful not to goad Dee in front of him, and to always be polite to her in his company.

Today Janet had received a text from Billy to say he was back in the UK, and to ask her to meet up with him about seven on Reculver beach. Billy's timekeeping wasn't that great, so the time was flexible. There were lots of cubby holes beneath the rocks on this rugged coastline, with just enough room for two people to squeeze inside. They both got a thrill out of having sex inside one, knowing that anyone could come along and see them, and be shocked. She knew the exact spot where he would be, so she returned his text to say she would be there to meet him.

She was very careful to make the best of herself. Her long hair glistened with its red highlights in the May sunshine, and she donned a very skimpy pair of shorts that showed off her legs and trim waist, and then she put on plenty of foundation to cover her spots. She had been very keen to see Billy soon, as she had some important news to share with him. If anyone had ever asked her if she loved Billy, she wasn't sure what her answer would be. Their on and off relationship was certainly full of passion, but she knew that Billy had a hot temper, and he could also be very arrogant, so she imagined he would not be an easy person to live with.

He could not remember his real mother, but he had told her he could never forgive her for having him adopted, even though she had parted from his father. His Dad belonged to the FBI, and had made contact with him, remaining a part of his life, and that was ironic because Billy had a few misdemeanours from his past with stealing cars and other petty crime.

Janet found herself a white sun top with a low neck to get him going, she hoped, and teamed it up with her shorts which showed off her tan. She left her long hair loose because Billy liked it that way, then made her way down towards the beach and their favourite cubby hole, feeling excited about seeing him again, whatever time he turned up.

Nathan was disappointed to find that Dee had locked herself in her bedroom when he got home. He had tapped on the door, intending to have a heart to heart chat with her, but there was no response. He sighed to himself, she was either asleep, or sulking inside, but because she was so touchy right now, he decided not to invade her space. He did try to connect with her.

"Dee, it's dad, come out and let's have a chat, we don't want to stop you going to the cinema, but doing revising as well is a good idea."

There was silence, so he went downstairs to see Lydia, putting his arm comfortingly around her.

"You did absolutely the right thing. She's getting to be such a madam, and she had done very little revision. I would have done the same, and when she deigns to open the door, I will tell her how disappointed I am in her attitude."

Lydia smiled gratefully at him. Nathan had always understood. He knew how lucky he was to have her. With her golden red hair and green eyes, she was truly beautiful. Having been a nurse in the past, she was capable and calm in the midst of many a crisis.

Knowing how much Nathan had suffered in the past, Lydia felt he didn't deserve all this as well. At the age of forty-two he still looked as handsome as when she first knew him, which was amazing, and his face bore no trace of trauma or stress, just a healthy glow. His hair was still thick, with no signs of baldness. He had definitely worn well.

"I am dishing up supper soon, so maybe when she smells the bacon, she might be tempted."

At that moment, Jack came down the stairs, two at a time, saying how starving he was, and they both laughed.

"Well, Jack's tempted," laughed Nathan. "Come on then, let's eat."

Dee and Beth were both still chuckling when they left the cinema after the film had ended. It was by now past six o'clock, and a beautiful mellow sunny evening. As they walked from the cinema, and crossed the road onto the promenade, they noticed that the tide had just turned and was now on its way out again.

"Shall we get some chips? I am starving!" remarked Dee.

"Good idea. We can eat them on the way home."

"Shall we get a couple of cans, too?"

"I was just about to suggest that; I am very thirsty," said Beth.

They walked past the bandstand, and crossed the road to get their chips. Dee was so grateful for this close friendship with Beth, her only friend. Whilst they were sitting in the cinema, she had seen several girls from their class. They had all acknowledged Beth, and Dee had stared back at them, hoping to get a smile as well, but no. Beth was probably the most popular girl in the school, and Dee was so glad they could see them together. Everybody loved Beth, but Beth had chosen her to go to the cinema with.

Dee found that the worst girl was Janet, but she wasn't there. Janet was the one who had slandered her mother's memory; the others just ignored her, and whispered in their own little clique. It was laughable that Janet was Billy's on and off girlfriend. How on earth had that happened? All she could hope for was that it wouldn't get serious.

It was hard to feel close to Billy. He was full of himself, and yet bitter at the same time because he hadn't known their mother. Maybe he had chosen Janet for his girlfriend to get back at her. But then she reasoned with herself, maybe Billy didn't know Janet taunted and bullied her. She was always polite in front of him on the rare occasions that they met up, and Dee had never told Billy about it.

They left the fish and chip shop. Dee was clutching the hot chips, and Beth had the cans of Sprite.

"Let's sit on the downs and eat," said Beth, as they passed the King's Hall.

"It's as close to home as I dare," laughed Dee, but in spite of her bravado, she was feeling wretched inside, knowing she had stepped badly out of line with Lydia. At this moment she didn't feel ready to confide in anyone. Her life was in turmoil right now, and she didn't know which way to turn.

After they had eaten their chips, they both had a few sips of their Sprite. Dee was very conscious of the fact that her house was just at the top of the downs, and she really hoped her deception hadn't been discovered. If so, her dad would be out looking for her. She didn't dare to go home yet, she had to wait until they all went to bed, and then slip in under the cover of darkness. She was sure if her dad had discovered what she had been up to he would have rung her phone, but that so far had remained silent. She had shut herself in her room before, and she was usually left to decide when she was ready to open the door and speak reasonably.

"I don't want to go home yet. I'll walk towards Reculver with you."

Beth wondered why that was. Had she had words at home? She best not probe. "OK, that sounds good," Beth agreed.

They walked along the promenade, which stretched down to

Thanet and beyond. Lots of people were out with young children, and dogs were running freely, enjoying the spring sunshine. Dee wanted to stop and drink her can all in one go, but Beth urged her to walk on. They had passed the village of Beltinge, when they unexpectedly met Janet and, because Beth was with her, Janet spoke to them.

"Did you enjoy the film?" she asked Dee, who looked at her in amazement. Why couldn't she always be like this? She didn't know what to say, but then Beth spoke up.

"It was very funny. We loved it!"

Janet had felt her heart sink when she met them. She didn't want anyone to spot her going to meet Billy; it was their special time together. She had to be nice to Dee right now because she was with Beth. No teasing or bullying, and no mention of her mother.

"Are you walking to your granny's house?" she asked Dee, holding her breath and hoping not, as then they would have to walk together. The beach was close, and Billy would be there soon. The promenade ended at Bishopstone, and the only way to Reculver, if you didn't want to walk along the beach at high tide and negotiate the rocks and cubby holes, was up the steps, and along the downs. Now that the tide had turned, and was slowly retreating, they wouldn't get cut off if they chose the beach.

"Not today. We are going to the downs, and then I will get my bus to Greenhill," said Beth, guessing that Janet was going to meet Billy and didn't want them around.

Beth lived on a fairly new housing estate at Greenhill, which was situated on the other side of the Thanet Way. Being able to walk on the downs overlooking the sea was a real treat for her.

They both said goodbye to Janet, and watched her walking towards the beach. No comment was made, but they both guessed that she was on her way to meet Billy. Beth flopped down on the grass, and offered to hold Dee's can whilst she went into the public toilet. After Dee came out, they both finished off their drinks. Beth felt a bit concerned about leaving Dee, but she had a pressing need to get home.

"Will you be OK if I get my bus now?" she asked.

"Of course, I will be fine."

Dee hid her anxiety well. She had a couple of hours at least left before it got dark, and nowhere particularly to go. But her pride stopped her from telling Beth, so she accompanied her to the bus stop at Reculver Road, and then waited with her until the bus arrived. The time was now just past seven, and for some reason that she could not comprehend, she started to feel a bit dizzy. She immediately blamed it on the fact that she was very close to the Headland, a piece of land which jutted out from the edge of Bishopstone Glen. Although it had happened ten years ago, she could still remember so clearly that day with Alice.

Alice had been her nanny, and had always been around as far back as Dee could remember, as well as her grandparents Philip and Isabel, and Nathan. When she had asked them about her mother, she had been told that her mummy was in hospital because she wasn't well, and one day she would be well enough to come back to her. And she had come back, and then Alice had left. But then Alice had returned to the house after Dee's birthday party, and told her that mummy had given her permission to take Dee on holiday. Because she was only six years old, and had always been close to Alice (she even called her Mumma Alice), she trustingly went with her.

They had stayed in a caravan that night, which at the time Dee had thought was fun because it was different. But the next morning she was missing her mother and wanted to go home. So Alice had taken her to Bishopstone Glen, which was where the Fairy Bridge was. She had always believed, at that age, that fairies lived under the bridge, and when she stood on the bridge, she had to listen out very carefully in case she might spot one. This was her favourite place to go.

But when Alice had spotted Sadie and Nathan there searching for Dee, Alice had reacted very strangely, holding Dee very tightly right at the edge of the cliff. That moment of absolute terror had never left Dee. But luckily Nathan had managed to grab her to safety, and it was Alice who had plunged over the side.

Sadie and Nathan had explained to her that Alice was not well, and Dee could believe that. Although she loved Alice, sometimes the tight way she held her, and the possessiveness she showed, had made her feel uncomfortable, and she had never forgotten the wild

25

b

look in her eyes, when she realised that Sadie and Nathan had caught up with her.

It might be ten years that had passed since then, but she found it hard to visit that glen, and had not walked along the headland path since that day. No wonder she felt a bit dizzy. But with the tide going out, if she returned to the beach, she could walk down to Reculver and back, and by then it would be getting dark.

She climbed over the rocks. The sand was still wet, but easy to walk on and she made herself look ahead as she passed Bishopstone beach. Oh, how she wished this dizziness and feeling of panic would pass. She was determined to beat it, so she urged her feet on, and her steps became quicker. She had by now passed the headland, so distinct as it jutted out to sea, but she was feeling even more dizzy and tired. She wondered if she was coming down with some nasty bug.

As she rounded the corner where the cliff face curved, who did she see but Billy. She then expected to see Janet with him, but he was alone. This part of the area was particularly rocky, and he was just coming from the back of the beach where the cliff formed small cave areas. He looked surprised to see her too.

"Hi sis, how're ya doing? I just got over for a small vacation. What are you doing here?"

His face seemed to be swirling towards her, and she could only gasp out: "Billy, I feel dizzy, help me."

"Try this." Billy took the cigarette out of his mouth, and placed it between her lips. "Take a drag."

Dee drew on it, anything to make her feel better. But it had the opposite effect. As she exhaled the smoke, dizziness overcame her, and his horrified eyes took in the sight of her crumpling to the ground completely unconscious.

Now Billy was filled with panic. He had only given her a puff of weed, and it had finished her off. It was supposed to give her the same lift it gave him. He knew he could be in big trouble for this. Looking around him, he could see the beach was deserted, so after unsuccessfully trying to rouse her, he dragged her unconscious body towards the cave entrance. She would be safe there, as the tide was going out.

He realised he couldn't use his mobile to get help for her. But, if he went back towards the glen, there was a red telephone box in Manor Road, and it still worked. Even though Billy had flouted the law in the past, he couldn't leave his half-sister unconscious on the beach.

Billy sped away and found the box, then dialled 999, and when the voice answered, he held his nose to mask his voice, and spluttered into the phone.

"A girl is lying on the beach between Bishopstone and Reculver, and she needs help!"

Chapter Three

Janet's meeting with Billy had not turned out the way she wanted it to. Part of his attraction was his non-conforming wildness, and the many risks that he took. She didn't think telling him she was pregnant would be much of a big deal. As she wanted to go into the sixth form at school, and then onto University, she had absolutely no plans to keep this baby, but she did feel it was right to let Billy know, because obviously they would have to be more careful next time. She did not feel at all maternal, and she knew her parents would not be thrilled to be grandparents in their early forties. They hardly noticed her, so a grandchild stood no chance.

When she had told Billy, his words still echoed in her mind.

"Well it's not mine. It could be anyone's, so don't try and lay the blame on me!"

He made her sound like the local bike! He had been her first lover, and at that moment she realised just how shallow he was. He had made her feel dirty and humiliated, and now she felt like she truly hated him.

"It's yours, Bill, but I wouldn't want to give birth to your child if you were the last man on earth!"

Strong words. But inside she didn't feel strong, she felt rejected. She left him, so that he wouldn't see her crying. He wasn't worth crying over, she told herself very firmly, but her heart argued back, and it hurt.

She hid herself amongst the rugged rocks. The tide was going out at the moment so anyone walking along the sand would be getting their feet wet, and it was no surprise to her that this part of the beach was empty. Notices were placed around the cliffs warning people about getting cut off at high tide, but in the past she had ignored them with Billy, it was fun taking risks and breaking rules she had thought. The walkers would all be up the top on the downs walking past Bishopstone in the direction of Reculver and The King Ethelbert pub.

She found a small cave, and sat down on a rock, not even caring that it was wet. She gave vent to her tears, and she knew her foundation was all streaked down her face. But what did it matter how she looked now, she had just been insulted by someone she thought might have cared a little about her. But clearly he had only wanted her for sex and, as far as he was concerned, to hell with the consequences!

Whilst she was sitting on the rock, she heard a noise behind her. Hope flooded through her that Billy had now got over the shock, and had come to apologise to her. So she turned to see who it was, but was not expecting to be hit on the back of the head, and as she fell forwards her forehead caught on a jagged rock and blood spurted out. Dazed and confused, her last coherent thought was wondering why they had done this to her, then she lost consciousness, and fell face forward into a rock pool.

After Billy's frantic call, it was decided to send the paramedics to the beach by helicopter, as there was no way they could have got an ambulance down onto the rocky area. The tide had only retreated a little way down the beach, and the sandy area was just beginning to be exposed. Whilst flying over, they hadn't spotted anyone lying on the sand, but it looked like there was an area with marks, as though a body had been dragged, and it led to the caves at the back.

Mark Sharp hovered the helicopter expertly high above the cliff edge, and his work partner Viv was winched down. She headed for the cave. By then Dee was stirring, semi conscious and muttering, so Viv quickly put a mask on to give her some oxygen, whilst speaking to her.

"Hello, my name is Viv, and I am a paramedic. Are you hurting anywhere?"

Dee shook her head, her eyes were full of confusion. Viv tried again.

"Can you tell me your name, and how you got into this area?"

It was all too much for Dee. She had a headache, and she was unaware of where she was. It was hard to remember anything. She closed her eyes again, retreating into the safety of darkness.

Viv moved swiftly, strapping Dee onto a stretcher, which was then attached to a lifting board and winched up into the helicopter. Viv turned to follow after, and then her eyes took in the cave next to where they had found Dee, which was just a few metres away. She spoke in to her intercom.

"Hang on, Mark, there is someone else down here, too."

But this time it was a much grimmer discovery. The body of a young girl in shorts was laying face downwards in a shallow rock pool. There was blood in the pool, which had clearly oozed out from her where she hit the rock, and from her neck, where a huge gash could be seen.

Viv turned her body over, but could see that any attempt to resuscitate was too late. She had died a while ago. It was clear that someone had hit her and then left her to drown in a rock pool. This poor girl had been murdered!

The appearance of the helicopter had caused quite a stir locally, so there were many curious people gathered at the top of the cliffs watching the proceedings. Word soon spread that two bodies had been winched up from the beach, and within no time at all, it had reached the local news desks and radio stations.

Nothing could be done to help Janet, so a blanket was placed over the body, but Dee was taken to the local hospital at Margate, and then wheeled straight into casualty. She was floating in and out of consciousness, and by the time they had found her a bed, they had also found her details and telephoned her home.

Nathan answered the telephone, scarcely believing what he was hearing. Lydia managed to find a spare key, and they were both mortified when they found Dee's room empty, and realised that Dee had gone to such lengths to get out. Normally they might have felt very angry about her deception, but right now all they could feel was anxiety and fear.

"I thought she wanted to go to the cinema. Why on earth was she on that beach, and who or what made her unconscious?" said Nathan. This was really worrying, whatever could possibly have happened to her?

"When we go and see her, we can find out," said Lydia soothingly, wondering if Dee had a boyfriend. Maybe that explained her desperation to get out. Lydia had no doubt that Nathan might find it hard to accept that Dee was growing up.

Lydia went upstairs to Jack's bedroom and told him, and he whistled with surprise.

"I saw the helicopter out of the window, but had no idea it was Dee. Is she OK?"

"We're off to find out now. Her dad is very worried. We had no idea she had gone out."

"I'm coming, too. She told me she wanted to go to the cinema."

They heard the phone ringing again, and Nathan answered it downstairs. By the time they had come down, he had replaced the receiver. He turned round and said, "Dee is awake now; let's get going and find out what's going on."

They all sat in silence whilst Nathan drove to the hospital, each wondering exactly what was going on. He parked the car, and they entered the casualty department. It was full of people sitting and waiting to be seen by a doctor.

Nathan enquired at the desk, and was told that Dee was in a small room at the end of the corridor. As they approached the door, they saw a nurse hovering outside. Nathan explained that they were Dee's family.

"Before you go in, doctor would like a quick word with you."

"Yes, of course," said Nathan, and a white coated doctor appeared.

"Good afternoon, Mr Edwards, I am Doctor Harvey. Do you know if your daughter Dee takes drugs at all?"

Nathan bridled with indignation. "Of course she doesn't. What a question!"

31

But as soon as he spoke the words, he realised that he didn't know. Dee had been acting very strangely for a couple of years now. Until then he thought he knew her inside out; she had always been a very open and sunny little girl, but then she had changed, and become a person who was very secretive. He couldn't bear to think his little girl was on drugs, how awful! They had nearly been his own downfall all those years ago. Thank God Philip had come along and rescued him by giving him a reason to turn his life around. By making him feel he was worth it, and not just a sad addict. He inwardly shuddered at the thought of it. Maybe now they would have to help Dee.

The doctor grimaced. "Your daughter is definitely suffering from stress, but she has some sort of drug in her system that we can't positively identify. Does she take any medication to help her to sleep, maybe an over the counter one from the chemist?"

Nathan and Lydia exchanged puzzled glances.

"Not that we know about," said Lydia. "We just thought she was suffering from teenage blues. She doesn't seem to be concentrating at school."

"Well they do tend to go a bit awry in their teens," agreed the doctor. "But maybe you could ask her if she has taken a sedative or sleeping pill. Otherwise, with no obvious injury, we can't find a reason why she was unconscious on the beach."

He moved away from the door, and they thanked him, and then they entered the little room. Dee was propped up on her pillows. She was awake, but her face was very pale, and when she saw them all, with concern written all over their faces, she started to sob, and guilt rushed through her at how much worry she must have caused them.

"Mummy, Daddy, I am so sorry, I truly am!"

Nathan crossed the room in a flash, folded her into his arms and let her sob. Lydia was there too, with her arm around Dee's shoulder. Jack stood there awkwardly; women's tears were a mystery to him.

"We are not angry with you. Whatever it is I can fix it," said Nathan, trying to show a confidence he didn't really feel. "But first the doctor has asked me to ask you, have you taken a sedative or sleeping pill, because apart from being very drowsy, they can't find any physical injury on you."

"I haven't, Daddy, truly I haven't. I have no idea why I felt so tired and dizzy."

"I guessed that," said Lydia. She knew that Dee didn't really like taking any pills. If she had any sort of pain or a headache, Dee tended to just ignore it. She didn't like being ill, and her health had never before been of any concern to them.

Dee trembled, and then gulped, she had to get it all off her chest; two years of misery stored up inside her, but threatening to erupt and drive her crazy at any time. She knew her family really didn't deserve the way she was taking her unhappiness out on them. Even if they couldn't do anything about it, at least she could tell them.

She took a deep breath and started to explain. As she went on it became easier to share, and the words came tumbling out. The ridiculing from the other girls, the hostility, and the vile accusations that had been made against her mother.

Nathan was aghast. How could anyone know such intimate details about Sadie's past? All the girls at Dee's school had been about two years old when Danny Foster had died. Anyone of Dee's age would not have known about what might have happened fourteen years ago; they must have heard it from a parent. Nathan and Lydia had been careful not to say anything.

Even he hadn't known everything about Sadie, as she had so many different sides to her character, but he had always believed her when she said that she had not killed Danny. And seeing as she had been in love with him at the time, and Dee was their daughter, Nathan could not see why Sadie would have killed him.

"Who is it that was taunting you?" he demanded.

"Daddy, she won't admit to it. For my sake, please don't say anything."

"Just tell me!"

Dee had never seen him so angry, and part of her rejoiced at the way he was trying to protect her. She had fought this battle on her own for too long.

"It was Janet. She found out about it from an old newspaper. She tried to suggest that my mother had murdered my real father."

"Your mother suffered from mental illness, and she was accused of murdering him, but it was never proved, and I personally believed her when she said she didn't do it. She was deemed not fit to stand trial because of her mental illness, so she went into a psychiatric unit. She had treatment, and then, as you know, she came home to be with you."

Nathan felt emotional as he said these words. The scars would never fully heal, although he could never put into words his gratitude to Lydia for making his life so much happier again, and becoming a stepmum to Dee. He felt it was important that Dee didn't have to carry the weight of her mother's past life on her young shoulders. Until recently, she had been a sunny, happy and uncomplicated girl. But now she had told them about the bullying, it explained a lot. He patted her hand comfortingly.

"Don't worry, we will sort it. You won't be bullied any more."

Jack had been listening to it all with great interest and was gobsmacked. He had no idea about all this; but girls were a mystery to him, the way they carried on. To him right now, they were an unknown species.

"Well, I have never been that keen on Janet. She is well matched with Billy. They both have hang ups, but you don't sis."

Dee smiled, she felt they were all on her side, and it seemed to help. But nobody had the right to vilify her mother!

"My mother was the best mother in the world. She couldn't help suffering from mental illness, lots of people do," she said with feeling.

"Of course she was!" said Lydia, squashing down any misgivings that she had. She knew that as far as Dee was concerned, the mother she had known had been warm and caring. Dee could remember when her granny had cancer and Sadie had stepped up, as Philip had not been able to face taking Isabel to hospital for her chemo sessions. She had gone with her every time, and kept her spirits up when she was low. After many uncomfortable years, Isabel had reunited with Sadie, and her lasting memories of her daughter were that she had saved her life, and helped her back to recovery again. There was no way that Nathan or Lydia would tarnish those precious memories; they would hold onto the secret they shared forever.

Dee suddenly had a thought. "Daddy, you mustn't come up to the school. It will only make it worse."

34

Nathan didn't have to respond to that, because at that moment the door opened and a nurse walked in.

"Are you feeling any better, Dee? Two policemen are outside, and they want to speak to you."

"Police?" echoed Nathan, and Jack let out a low whistle. "Why do they want to speak to her, Dee hasn't committed a crime?"

"I can't remember much," said Dee, also wondering why they had come.

A silence fell as the door opened to admit two policemen. They were both in uniform, which must have caused quite a stir, aged about mid-thirties, and their faces showed empathy, but also a determination to do their job. The taller one spoke first.

"Good evening, Miss Edwards, can we call you Dee?"

Dee nodded silently.

They introduced themselves to Nathan and Lydia, and nodded at Jack too.

"We understand you were found unconscious on the beach, and you can't remember how you got there."

"My head feels fuzzy. I just remember going for a walk after Beth went home."

"Beth is your friend from school?"

"That's right, my best friend." She could have added her only friend, but she didn't want to go through it all again, and there was something in their manner that made her feel cautious.

"We went to the cinema, I do remember that, but I don't even remember being on the beach."

The two policemen exchanged glances, and Nathan and Lydia were now totally mystified and wondered what exactly was going on.

"You were found in a small cave at the back of the beach. There were marks in the sand to indicate you fainted further down the beach and someone dragged you into the cave. Were you aware of anyone else being there, nearby to you?"

This sounded even more involved to Nathan. Who had dragged Dee's body up the beach? He could see the questioning was getting a bit too much for her.

"Dee has told you she doesn't remember being there. What is this all about?"

"Well, Mr Edwards, it's about a girl from the same school as Dee being found dead on the beach, just a few yards away from her. She had been hit on the back of the head, and left to die in a shallow pool."

Fear coursed through Nathan. Maybe the murderer had also moved Dee up the beach, but then commonsense took over. Surely moving her up the beach made her safer from the tide, but who on earth would have done that?

"Which girl?"

"Now that her parents have been informed, we can release her name: Janet Philpott."

Nathan felt cold fingers clutching at his heart. The girl who had made Dee's life a misery had been murdered on the beach, and Dee had been found unconscious nearby without any apparent memory of it. Any normal person could have snapped with that sort of pressure on them. Whoever had moved her up the beach had obviously wanted to protect her, but who was it, and what the hell was going on?

"Have you any idea who moved Dee up the beach when she fainted?"

"Not yet, sir. But the incident was reported from a local phone box in Manor Road, so they obviously didn't want to use their mobile, which means they had something to hide, and we will find them!"

Nathan had no doubt that they would, but with Dee unwittingly involved, it felt too close to home. Oh, why was it, he wondered, that this family could never be free of drama?

Chapter Four

The doctors had decided to keep Dee in hospital overnight. They had come to the conclusion, that unbeknown to her parents, she must have taken an over the counter sleeping medication. The whys and wherefores of the reason she had done it, was not up to them, but the police, to decide. By the morning, she would not be feeling so sleepy and would have recovered from her shock. Various tests had shown there was nothing else wrong with her, so, when the doctor signed her off in the morning, she would be free to go home.

After reassuring her that everything would be all right, Nathan, Lydia and Jack finally left her, arriving home at eleven o'clock. It was not surprising that there was a message from a very anxious Beth on the answerphone. Nathan took a chance on the lateness of the hour, and rang her back.

"Hello Beth, thanks for ringing. Dee is OK, just a bit sleepy, and she should be coming home tomorrow."

"I heard all about the helicopter, and I couldn't believe it was Dee. We had been to the cinema together, and then she came to the bus stop with me, and waited with me until my bus came. It must have happened soon after that."

"Yes, and it's very sad about Janet. Did you know she was upsetting Dee with stories about her mother which are not true?"

"Yes, Dee told me. She was very angry and upset. The other girls started to ignore her too, and she got some nasty comments on her Facebook page, so she deleted it."

Nathan guessed that for a sixteen year old to not have a Facebook page probably felt tragic; all teenagers wanted to be in the loop together, nobody wanted to be the odd one out. His heart ached for Dee. If only they had realised how much she was suffering. But more importantly right now, was the realisation that she was in some way connected with the murder on the beach, and that was very worrying.

"It sounds like Janet was a girl who liked upsetting others, which means that anyone could have murdered her, although it is certainly very tragic," he remarked.

"Well, she certainly enjoyed upsetting Dee. But I have always defended her, and I always will, she is my closest friend," said Beth with feeling.

"I know, and we are so grateful for your loyalty. So many teenagers can be led like sheep just to ensure that they personally don't lose their popularity. I am sure Dee would love to see you if you can come round tomorrow."

"Oh yes, thanks so much, I will come round tomorrow afternoon. Please give her my love when you see her, and tell her I am on her side."

As Nathan returned the telephone to its rest, Janet's words echoed in his head. They were all on Dee's side, she had done nothing wrong. He was aware that the police were good at insinuating things, but he didn't believe that Dee had it in her to hurt anyone. Somebody else had killed Janet. . . maybe the person who had dragged Dee's body up the beach; and another thought struck him, leaving her so close to Janet would arouse the suspicions of the police, so maybe that person had wanted to frame her.

After her family had left, Dee tried to collect her jumbled thoughts. The relief she felt at finally admitting that she had been bullied was tempered with the horror she felt at knowing Janet was dead. She hadn't liked her at all, but she would never have wished anything nasty on her. And the police had made her feel very guilty. It wasn't her fault that Janet had died very close to where she was found unconscious. Surely the police didn't think she was in league with the person who had dragged her body up the beach? It was a scary thought that someone had done that anyway, and she hoped they would find out who it was.

She tried to rack her brains in an effort to remember what had happened yesterday. The film had been funny, and she could remember seeing other girls from her class there, then she remembered walking along the seafront with Beth. They had bought some chips, but all she could remember after that was going to the bus stop with Beth, and waiting to see her onto her bus. She had felt stressed because she was quite close to Bishopstone Glen where Alice had met her death. When had she gone on the beach? And Billy, hadn't she seen him somewhere, or had she imagined it? She felt like her mind was playing tricks on her, but that fear of being near to the glen was so strong. It wasn't that far from the bus stop, and it had been a while since she had been up that way, usually only passing through by car on the way to her grandparents' house.

She really had thought that she had got it all out of her system, but all the stress she had suffered from Janet seemed to have heightened her fears again. She admitted to herself that, although she was mortified to hear that Janet had died, part of her was relieved that her main troublemaker could not upset her any more. The other girls, she felt, just followed their leader. They had no backbone, except Beth. Beth was amazing, she was such a close friend, but nobody ostracised her because of it. It seemed that, because of her sunny nature, she had the ability to get on with everyone. But then it seemed that Beth didn't have any skeletons in her cupboard.

Dee remembered back to the first time she had met her mother; she had been so shy, she had hidden behind a curtain. She knew her mother had been ill, and would come home one day, and until then the people who had remained constant in her life, and given her such emotional security, had been her beloved grandparents, Nathan, who always felt like her dad, and Alice. But as soon as she met Sadie, she felt such a strong connection to her, not just because she looked like her, but because she had so much admiration for her.

She had seen nothing but good in her mother, including her helping granny to get well when she was struck down with cancer.

39

Poor Philip had fallen apart, he couldn't bear the fact that Isabel was so ill, and he had his own fear of hospitals.

Dee remembered how much love Sadie had shown her. She was always there for her, she could talk to her, and they had shared some fun times together. It was for less than two years that her mother had been a part of her life, but it had been her happiest time. When Sadie married Nathan, her happiness was complete, she felt she had a mother and a father, but it had been so short-lived. She could never forget the day Nathan had to tell her that her mother had been killed in a road accident.

The next year had been hell for the whole family, but then Lydia had come along and helped her to get through it. She didn't want to think of Nathan always being on his own, so when he asked her if she minded if he married Lydia, she understood that life had to go on, and she was relieved because Lydia had become important to her.

In her mind, no one could take her mother's place, but Lydia had never tried to, she had just been there to support her and Nathan. She could remember there had been angry words between herself and Lydia yesterday; if only she had found the courage to admit to Lydia that she wanted to show others in her class, that in spite of all the bullying, she did have one loyal friend.

Dee was filled with a new determination now. She vowed that when she got home she would give back as good as she got at school. She would tell them that the person they were reviling was not her mother, but a made up person, and most importantly, she would be kinder to Lydia, because even though she was not her blood mother, she was a good and kind person, who deserved her respect. With all that now off her conscience, she plumped up her pillow and settled down to go to sleep.

The next morning, it was eleven o'clock before the doctor had completed his rounds. Dr Harvey gave his permission for her to return home. Today she felt much more clear headed, to her relief, because yesterday she felt like she had been floating along like a zombie, not quite registering everything that was said to her. However, her memory was still vague about collapsing on the beach, although she did remember seeing Billy. Then a terrifying

40

thought struck her; surely Billy hadn't killed Janet? Had she seen them together? She really wasn't sure. Billy had a bit of a past. He had often boasted about it; he had stolen cars and been involved in petty crime in America, and his father and adopted parents had hoped when he came to England, and met his grandparents and sibling, it would help him to realise it wasn't the way to behave.

His adopted parents Simon and Jill Hopkins loved him very much, but it seemed they weren't enough for Billy. He quite liked the idea that his real dad was an FBI man, it was something to boast about. But as soon as she thought about it, Dee thrust the idea right out of her mind. Billy wasn't a murderer, just a young man trying to grow up, and suffering from insecurity. And, after all, he was her brother.

She sent Nathan a text to say she could now go home, and it wasn't long before he arrived to pick her up.

"How do you feel today?" he enquired, as she hugged him warmly.

"Much better, Daddy, my head is not so fuzzy, and my headache has gone, too."

"That's good because Beth is coming round to see you this afternoon."

This news made her feel better already. She was grateful for Beth's loyalty. Dee planned to tell her that she was going to stand up to the hostility, she was absolutely determined. But she wondered what sort of atmosphere there would be at school now that Janet had passed away.

As if reading her thoughts, Nathan spoke.

"As you can imagine, the news about Janet is everywhere, on the news, in the papers, and there is all sorts of speculation. People are nervous about letting their children go on the beach, and we feel the same about you. We want you to be safe, so if you do go, please don't go alone. I know you are sixteen, almost an adult, but there is always safety in numbers, and hopefully it won't be too long before the police discover who committed this terrible crime."

"Yes, Daddy, I understand. To be honest, I don't feel much like going to the beach at the moment."

"The school is open this morning, even though it's a weekend, and the police are interviewing all the girls to see if anyone knows anything."

"They are bound to want to interview me again," Dee said gloomily. She had not enjoyed the interrogation.

"Yes, but not today! Nathan said firmly. "They saw you last night, and you have been through enough."

When they arrived home, Lydia hugged her warmly, which reminded Dee that she hadn't been very nice to her yesterday. Her apology came from her heart.

"I am so sorry I argued with you yesterday, I wish now that I hadn't gone out."

Lydia guessed she was thinking that if she hadn't gone out, then she wouldn't have been anywhere near the murder scene. She hastened to reassure her.

"I wouldn't worry, I am sure it will all be OK in the end. Now come and try to eat some salad."

Dee didn't feel that hungry. Anxiety seemed to destroy her appetite, but she managed to eat a bowl of tuna salad. Lydia knew it was her favourite, and had prepared it specially. There was no way that Nathan and Jack would eat something like that for lunch, but both Lydia and Dee liked it.

Dee thanked her, realising just how much she took Lydia for granted. Lydia spent all her time trying to please them all, and shame coursed through her at her behaviour the previous day, although it seemed Lydia just wanted to put it behind them. She thanked her, and after she had finished, she put her bowl in the dishwasher.

A few minutes later, the doorbell went, and she heard Lydia welcoming Beth in. Seeing her cheered Dee immensely, the two girls hugged warmly, and then they were left alone to chat in the conservatory.

"How are you feeling today? I was so shocked to hear you were in hospital," said Beth.

"I am OK today. But honestly, Beth, I don't remember going on that beach, and I had no idea Janet was there."

"You don't have to convince me of your honesty. It's weird to think we saw her not long before she died. I think she was going to meet Billy," mused Beth.

42

"I can't remember seeing her at all. I am not sure if I imagined it or not, but I thought I spoke to Billy somewhere. Just Billy, she wasn't with him."

"I am sure the police will speak to him. He's just as much a suspect as anyone else. I was interviewed at school this morning, along with the rest of the class, and they took our fingerprints. I am sure they will want you to confirm that you saw me get on the bus. You do remember that, don't you?"

"Yes, it's what happened afterwards that I am confused about, partly because I had to walk past Bishopstone Glen. It was my first time up there for years."

"Oh yes, of course, the place where your nanny died. Dee, you probably can't remember because of the stress that causes you. It might all come back later."

"Maybe, but I do hope the police won't think I killed her because she was bullying me. I am sure the other girls interviewed will have told them that."

"Dee, I don't believe you could even kill a fly, don't worry. Whatever people think they know about your mother does not mean that you are a bad person."

Beth gave her another hug to lift her sombre mood, and Dee wondered how she would ever manage without her. Beth to her was a beautiful person, inside and out; with her sparkling blue eyes, her sincerity always shone through.

"You always make me feel so much better!" she said, with feeling.

Chapter Five

DCI Alan Clarke was sitting at his desk in Wimbledon police station, when the telephone rang out imperiously. Ever since his son Adam had been born, he couldn't stop thinking about how proud he felt. Zoe was such an amazing woman, and he was so grateful that he had been there, holding her hand and urging her on, when Adam had entered the world some six weeks before.

To an onlooker Adam had looked like most newborn babies, with his head a little misshapen after delivery and only thin wisps of downy hair lying flat against his scalp. His face had been red, and he had aired his lungs shortly after delivery, just to let the world know that he had arrived. But just like any proud father, to Alan he was beautiful. After one year of marriage, there were now three of them, and he couldn't be happier.

At six weeks old, his face had now filled out, and his head had now recovered from the trauma of childbirth. His silver blond hair seemed to have a kink in it; it was now sprouting in all directions, and to Alan he looked exactly like a miniature version of his mother, which endeared him to his father even more. He was convinced that his son had smiled at him when he held him last night, even though Zoe had said he might have wind.

Although Alan's job was a demanding one, which took him away from home quite frequently, he had not been absent when Zoe went into labour. It was on a Sunday, the first one he had to himself for over a month, and his son had dutifully obliged them both by being born that evening, after Zoe had been in labour since early morning.

He had taken a week of his annual leave to be with her. Becoming parents had been a life changing experience for both of them, and he was so glad he had been around to share the birth with her. Seeing Zoe in such pain had been distressing, and at that point he had felt so useless, but as soon as she started pushing, he had held her hand and encouraged her every step of the way.

When he saw his son's head emerging, and then he was finally delivered, Alan was there to welcome him into the world. It had been a special moment, and his love and admiration for Zoe, knowing all she had been through, tied the bonds of love between them even tighter. He felt privileged to have been able to share the birth with her.

He had marvelled at how easily Zoe had taken to motherhood. Her previous experience of being a nurse had stood her in good stead, caring for her son came naturally, and her placid and calm nature helped her to cope.

In return, Adam slept from one feed to the next, and the only time when he was a bit restless was during the early evening, when he seemed to have wind and wanted to be held. Not that Alan minded that, he liked nothing more than holding his son when he arrived home from work. Zoe needed her hands free to get dinner, and she had explained to him that Adam was suffering from colic, a very common condition in new born babies, which would gradually fade away when his digestive system became more able to cope, which was usually at about three months old.

He interrupted his reverie to answer the telephone.

"Good morning, DCI Clarke here."

"Good morning, Clarke, Chief Superintendent Kevin Watts here. I am coming over later. There is something I need to discuss with you."

Alan's curiosity was roused. He didn't know the Chief Superintendent that well, but as he covered a large area, and was a very important man, it meant if he was coming over to this police station, then something major was going on.

"Nothing wrong, I hope, sir?"

"Not at all, but I will explain it all when I get there."

This was even more mystifying to Alan. He had only met this man once before, and that had been just after the case two years ago, when a suspect murderer had kidnapped Zoe and the young PC Wendy Stuart. The whole case had been a very dramatic one, as the suspect had a dual personality and had turned out to be a person with severe mental illness.

He still remembered the fear he had felt when Zoe disappeared, and then the knowledge that the suspect was completely out of control and wanted to harm Zoe. It turned out that this psychopath had previously murdered Eleanor Harrison, a very well known celebrity.

It had been a most difficult case to solve, and Alan didn't feel he could take any credit for discovering the murderer. He had been helped by a very astute police constable, who had kept a cool head and given Alan the support he needed when he felt like he was falling apart. With Zoe being kidnapped, the case was just too close to home.

The constable had played a prominent part in the rescue of Zoe, and showed himself to be a reliable member of the force. The murderer ended up committing suicide, which was a sad outcome for someone respected in their own working life in which they had showed no signs of a split personality or other mental illness.

Alan had been pleased that such a prominent murder case had finally been solved. The constable concerned had recently relocated to another branch, so now Alan had the constable's ex-partner Wendy working alongside him. They had a good working relationship. Wendy was uncomplicated and easy to get on with. She also got on well with Zoe, and made such a fuss of Adam when Zoe brought him to the office, thus endearing her even more to Alan and Zoe.

Wendy had gone to get some coffee for them both, so Alan unwrapped his sandwiches. Zoe was on a health kick, and his usual white bread had been changed to brown with seeds in it, and his cheese sandwich was accompanied by a salad, all carefully chopped up small with a light dressing on it.

"Oh no, I have got weeds again," he remarked, staring disdainfully at the unapologetic lettuce.

Wendy handed him his coffee. "Lettuce is good for you," she said, grinning. "Look, I also have salad in my sandwich."

In spite of his protestations, Alan liked the feeling that Zoe was taking care of him. Before they had moved in together, and subsequently got married, he had takeaways every lunchtime, and he knew they were not good for him. Lately he had lost weight without needing to go to the gym, so his little lady was actually doing him proud.

"I just had a call from Chief Superintendent Kevin Watts. He's coming over to see us, so we best eat up quickly."

"Where is he coming from?"

"Well, he works at New Scotland Yard."

"Wow, I wonder why he is coming?"

"Exactly what I thought. It must be important. Did you meet him when he was here before, eighteen months or so back?"

"I think so. A tall man with silver grey hair, about early fifties."

"Yes. He's the one. He commended Roger for his support in the Eleanor case."

He didn't need to explain any more to her, it was a case that would be impossible for either of them to forget, and they were temporarily plunged into silence as they relived the horror of it.

They ate their lunch and then drank their coffee, both remembering that discovering the suspect had been corrupt, and a murderer, had shocked. There was also some guilt, as is often the case after such a traumatic event, when families have been estranged since early childhood and the children have suffered at the hands of their mother, leading to a lack of stability or any sort of normal life, all of which may well have contributed to the suspect's mental problems. Whether or not the suspect's own sad suicide could have been prevented had they confided in someone, no one knew.

After they had finished eating, Wendy collected up the cardboard containers to dispose of them. As someone important was coming, she went into the ladies toilet to clean her teeth and renew her lipstick. She also gave Alan a mint to suck.

Feeling a bit nervous, she glanced around the office to make sure it looked tidy enough for a visitor. Alan, as usual, had a pile of papers and files on his desk, so she took the opportunity, when he left the room for a few minutes, to tidy them up. She smiled to herself, knowing that when he returned he would protest that it was so tidy that he couldn't find anything.

After Alan returned, he had no time to protest, as the duty constable tapped on the door to let them know that the Superintendent had arrived, and he would be with them very shortly.

"He might want to speak to you privately," she reminded Alan.

"Well, let's wait and see," he replied.

Chief Superintendent Watts was a powerful force, who dominated the room from the moment he entered. Wendy's description of a tall man with silver grey hair was accurate, and his presence was very strong; his grey eyes did not miss a thing. He held out his hand to Alan.

"Good afternoon, Clarke. Congratulations, I hear you have a son now. Good afternoon, young lady, I think I have met you before."

Wendy almost curtsied to him, it felt like she was in the presence of royalty. Her reply was deferential.

"Good afternoon, sir. Yes, I am WPC Wendy Stuart. I used to partner Roger Weston. He has transferred, and now I partner DCI Clarke."

"Well, in that case you need to hear what I have to ask."

Wendy and Alan exchanged glances, this was most intriguing.

"How old are you, Clarke?"

Alan had been about to thank him for mentioning his son, but realised that the conversation had ended on that subject, and it was now down to business. Wendy might like hearing more about Adam, and his progress, but the Chief Superintendent Watts had just been polite, and now wanted to discuss something else.

Alan had realised for a while now, that becoming a father had softened him up. That was fine at home, but at work he had to retain his businesslike image.

"Twenty-nine, sir," he said, wondering why he had been asked such a question.

"And you, Miss Stuart?"

"Twenty-five, sir."

"So fourteen years ago, your ages would have been eleven and fifteen."

They both nodded, and the superintendent went on to explain.

"There was a very high profile case in which the famous footballer Danny Foster was found dead in his swimming pool. After lengthy investigations, the coroner recorded an open verdict. Some say he committed suicide because he was just about to be dropped from the team. Others think it was an accident, as he couldn't swim, and he had been drinking and was well over the limit. At the time the police believed he might have been murdered. He had an affair, and the woman became pregnant. He didn't want to know about this child, so it was believed that the woman murdered him for revenge."

"Oh yes, I do remember!" exclaimed Alan. Although he was only fifteen at the time, he remembered the face of the woman accused of the murder being splashed over every newspaper. How could anyone forget that sultry beauty, with her very dark hair and eyes, and such an air of mystery about her?

"I just can't think of the accused woman's name," he exclaimed.

"Sadie Morton Brown."

"That's it. She was found unfit to stand trial, and went into a psychiatric unit."

"She was, in fact, incarcerated for four years, but after various treatments, it was believed she was no danger to society. So she was released."

Alan was finding this very interesting. "What happened to her then?"

"When she came out, she went back to live with her parents, who had by now moved to Herne Bay. It was said she was a changed woman. She had become religious, too. She bonded with her daughter and started to live a normal life by reconciling with her mother, and then marrying Nathan Edwards and moving to Canterbury. But her new life was short lived. Tragedy struck, and she was killed in a road accident, hit by a van."

"Oh, what a tragedy!" echoed Alan, as Sadie Morton Brown had captured his imagination.

"I don't remember any of it," confessed Wendy. This was the year she had taken her eleven-plus examination and her focus was

49

on passing it, and she hadn't even thought about being in the police force.

"Well, the reason I am telling you all this is because a murder has been committed, and we need to revisit that family again. Sadie's daughter, who now calls herself Dee, and has been adopted by Nathan, Sadie's widower, has also taken his surname, which is Edwards."

"Is it her daughter Dee that has been murdered?"

"Oh no, Dee is alive and well, but she was found unconscious on the beach near to another girl who had been murdered."

"Wow, so do you think it's a coincidence that it has happened within the same family? But Sadie was never actually convicted of the murder, was she?"

"Sadie's intentions will always remain a mystery to us. Dee professes to not remember how she got on the beach, and it looks like a third person dragged her unconscious body up the beach so she wouldn't drown when the tide turned and came in again. That person also raised the alarm by phoning from a local call box."

"A call box?" said Alan.

"Yes, they were obviously trying to hide their identity, but we have their fingerprints. We just need to match them up."

"I see. Was that the case where she was airlifted to hospital? I do remember reading about that."

"Yes, and they couldn't find anything wrong with her, apart from her being a bit drugged up. A girl from her class, Janet Philpott, was found at the same time that Dee was airlifted, just a few yards away from her. Janet had been hit over the head with a rock, and she fell face downwards then drowned in a shallow pool."

"So you think Dee killed her?" said Alan, in amazement.

"I am not saying that, but it doesn't add up, and we need to identify the person who moved her up the beach. Maybe they did it, and were trying to frame her."

"Has Dee got a motive to kill Janet?"

"She does, because Janet found out about her mother's infamous past, and taunted her with it."

"So Janet was a bully, which means she could have had other enemies."

Chief Superintendent Watts could see that his information was whetting Alan's appetite to find out more. His curiosity was aroused, which is what he had wanted to happen.

"Absolutely right, and there is also a half-brother called Billy. Sadie was married briefly when she went to America, but had him adopted. His existence came to light after Sadie died, and his father turned up in the UK. In recent years Billy has travelled between England and the States. Sadie's parents, Philip and Isabel, have him to stay with them quite often, and he just happens to be the boyfriend of deceased Janet."

"It sounds a very interesting case, but how sad that a teenage girl was murdered," said Wendy.

"Yes, her parents are devastated. They both have very busy professional lives, so now blame themselves for not having more time to spend with her."

"Yes, very sad. So the culprit must be found!" said Alan, with great determination.

"How would you feel about covering the case? Both of you, of course."

Wendy glanced doubtfully at Alan. He had already regaled her with tales of how he loved to come home from work and hold Adam every evening. It had been nice to see a softer side to him, because in this job, it paid to keep a stiff upper lip. So many tragic things happened, and it was hard sometimes not to take it home with you.

She realised it was a couple of hours journey to Herne Bay, so even if they travelled there daily, they wouldn't get home until eight o'clock. It didn't matter to her, she was single, and would go anywhere that she was sent because her job was important to her. But Alan wouldn't want to leave Zoe so soon after Adam's birth.

His next words took her totally by surprise. "I don't know how Wendy feels, but I am not keen on travelling backwards and forwards every day. My in-laws have moved to Whitstable and, if it was convenient, we could stay with them, but I would want to check with Zoe first."

Chief Superintendent Watts turned to Wendy enquiringly. "We would make sure we put you into a nice comfortable hotel, all expenses paid, of course."

51

"That sounds fine to me. Yes, I would be prepared to go with DCI Clarke," said Wendy politely. She was thinking how nice it would be to get away from the hustle and bustle of London, and enjoy some time in the sea air at the coast. It was a very sensitive case, with a young girl involved, and a grieving family, so the sooner they could solve it, and give the poor dead girl's parents closure, the better. She could feel great empathy for them already.

"Splendid!" The superintendent beamed triumphantly. "When you confirm it with me, Clarke, you will be filled in with the details we have so far."

Chief Superintendent Watts shook hands with both of them, and then left the room. He knew that young Clarke had the reputation of being a dedicated police officer, who had a balance in his approach which included meticulous professionalism coupled with empathy. His young partner had also proved herself, not only to be empathetic towards grieving families, but also strong-minded without being full of herself. On the surface she appeared to be a quiet person, but she had proved in the past that she was willing to speak out about injustice, and fight for it if necessary. He remembered back to the Eleanor Harrison case, some eighteen months ago, as if anyone could forget that one. She had made sure that Peter Grant got justice, and insisted that he wasn't judged because he had Asperger's Syndrome.

He was aware that it had been a failing of the police force in the past, to assume that anyone who appeared different, must have committed a crime. But that young lady would have none of it, and it had made them realise that in future things had to change, and people should not be judged because they were different.

This particular crime was a harrowing one. It was always very sad when a teenager died, whether through intention or accident; a life lost before it had scarcely begun. But Chief Superintendent Kevin Watts was confident that DCI Clarke and WPC Wendy Stuart were the right team to solve this case.

Chapter Six

"Oh, Alan, I am so glad you are home. Adam just won't go down."

Zoe ran her fingers distractedly through her curly blonde hair, making it stand out even more than usual. She had no make-up on, and was flushed and agitated, but she bore the glow that is bestowed by mother nature on new mothers, and, to Alan, she never looked more beautiful.

"OK, let me hold him," Alan said soothingly, and she gently transferred Adam and his blanket into his arms.

Alan looked proudly at his son. His very blue eyes were just like his mother, and the white blond hair was gradually thickening and becoming curly. He fixed his eyes on his father, then drawing up his legs he let out a wail of discomfort.

"He's very windy," remarked Zoe.

Alan held him against his shoulder as he had seen Zoe do many times, and gently patted his back. When nothing happened he started to walk slowly up and down, so Zoe took the opportunity to put a meat pie in the oven and quickly prepare some vegetables.

Since Adam had been born, Alan had discovered a patience he didn't realise he had. He could sense that Zoe was a bit vulnerable at the moment, and for her this was the most difficult time of the day with Adam. He had come home a bit later one evening to find her in tears, and his son loudly airing his lungs. It made him realise just how much they both needed him, and since then he had done his utmost to get home from work on time. It may well be that this colic problem would only last another six weeks, but to Zoe, so soon after childbirth, it must seem like a lifetime.

"I think he needs changing," he commented, when a familiar odour rose up. Zoe turned from the oven looking harassed, but he soon reassured her. "Don't worry. I can change him, just concentrate on dinner."

Zoe was relieved when Alan left the room to change Adam. She felt that because she was a nurse everyone expected her to make a perfect mother and be able to cope easily. She had worked hard to let Alan think she was coping, but in truth, at this time of day, nothing could help Adam settle, and it made her feel helpless and hopeless. She so wanted everything to be running smoothly when Alan came in from work. She knew he had a very stressful job and deserved time to unwind. But it seemed that they couldn't sit down and eat dinner together, because Adam had other ideas.

It was amazing that when his dad held him he did settle down and, as she was breastfeeding, after his last feed about eleven, he did sleep round until about six o'clock in the morning. But dinner time was often disrupted, as neither of them wanted to leave him crying. She was cooking the pie and mash in the hope that Adam would sleep on until they had eaten it.

She concentrated on cooking the dinner, knowing that Adam was in safe hands. And to her immense relief, when it was ready to be dished up, Alan came downstairs very quietly with a thumbs up sign.

"He's gone off. How great that it's ready," he remarked, and then helped her to carry the full plates into the dining room.

Zoe had made the meat pie earlier in the day whilst Adam was asleep. She wanted to please Alan in case he felt a bit left out since Adam had been born. Home-made steak pie was his favourite, and she was glad that just for once their meal was not interrupted.

"This is lovely. Your pies are to die for!" said Alan, very enthusiastically tucking into his dinner.

Zoe smiled and started to cut a piece off, only to hear the familiar indignant wail of their son echoing from the baby monitor. She jumped out of her chair, telling Alan not to let his dinner get cold, and went upstairs. Suddenly it all became too much for her, and she burst into tears, forgetting that Alan could hear everything through the baby monitor.

His dinner temporarily forgotten, Alan's long legs took the stairs two at a time, and he wrapped Zoe into his arms, whilst Adam's complaining became louder.

"Honey, whatever is wrong? He has to air his lungs sometime. I will hold him whilst you eat your dinner. You look all in."

"I wanted you to enjoy your dinner. I made that pie especially for you."

Alan stroked her hair soothingly, and she raised her tear-stained face to him.

"I am enjoying the pie, but you haven't even started yours yet."

He moved over to the cot and gathered Adam into his arms, and the baby immediately stopped crying. Now his voice became authoritative. She looked so wretched, and his heart went out to her. Maybe tough love was the answer.

"There is nothing wrong with him, Zoe. Now we are going down. You will eat your dinner; afterwards I can finish mine. It can be kept warm in the oven. "

Zoe didn't argue. She felt tired. Not just tired, in fact, exhausted, and very hungry, as she had been on her feet all day. She watched him walking around with Adam whilst she ate her dinner. Afterwards they swapped over, and Zoe watched him demolishing a large piece of meat pie.

As was usual, they spent the rest of the evening until the last feed taking it in turns to hold and play with Adam. It was a time that Alan really enjoyed, as he felt he was getting to know his son even more. Zoe fed him at eleven o'clock, and then tucked him up for the night. This gave them the opportunity to speak to each other. Zoe had by then composed herself.

"I am very sorry I got upset. I know that I am lucky that we have such a healthy baby boy, and during the day I can cope, but when you come in everything seems to fall apart. I am not suggesting that it's your fault, but at that time of the day I want to spend time with you, and Adam won't let me."

"I know, but it's not forever, he's only six weeks old. Zoe, you are everything to me, and you are being so hard on yourself. Whilst we are going through this difficult patch, as much as I loved it, I don't expect you to make meat pies. The supermarkets are full of ready meals, which will be quicker and easier for you. You can get back to home cooking when he's a bit older."

Zoe looked aghast. Had she really been trying too hard? "I didn't think you liked ready meals."

"Right now we need everything to be simple, ready meals will be fine," said Alan firmly. "I think you have the baby blues, but I have something to ask you, and this might help you at this time. But, of course, if you don't want to do it, you only have to say."

Zoe wondered what was coming next; with Alan's job you never knew.

"I don't want to go abroad."

"Of course not honey, neither do I right now. You remember you mentioned your parents were looking forward to us visiting them. . ."

"Yes, but you had a week off only recently. I wasn't expecting to be able to go just yet."

"I have been asked to do an assignment in Herne Bay."

"Oh Alan, of course, the girl on the beach who was murdered. They want you to solve it."

"Yes, with Wendy, but there is no way that I could travel there and back each day. So if your parents would like us to come and stay, your mum would be an extra pair of hands to help you with Adam, and cook dinner."

Suddenly Zoe felt like a great big weight had been taken off her shoulders. She knew her parents would be thrilled to have them to stay, and they could then spend more time with Adam. She felt that life was becoming great again now that big knot of worry had been removed from her mind. Her face broke out into a smile.

"Alan, that is great. I will give Mum a ring in the morning and arrange it all."

Kevin Watts took a sip of brandy after a very satisfying meal, and his thoughts wandered as he recalled his conversation with Alan Clarke earlier that day. The case had to be handled with a great deal of sensitivity. Interviewing teenagers was never easy. They thought at that age that death was a long way in the future, and it should be; assuming they were invincible. So when something like this happened it was very traumatic, and it made them feel frightened and insecure. There would probably have to be counselling offered to them. Herne Bay was an area where news got around very quickly because so many people knew each other in that small area, and the shock that such a lovely seaside town had been the place where a murder had taken place would resound everywhere.

Whether the Morton Brown girl was involved had to be investigated, and it would be wrong to suspect her because of her mother's dubious past, so they must be careful not to jump to conclusions.

Then there was the half-brother, who was Janet's boyfriend. A phone call had come through to Kevin confirming that Janet had been about six weeks pregnant. He wondered whether Billy or her parents had known about it. Billy was known to have a quick temper, but would he have murdered her because she was pregnant? If that was so, then he was evil and heartless. Janet didn't appear to have many friends at school except Beth, the golden haired girl with the innocent eyes. She was Dee's friend as well as Janet's. A girl with a big heart, it seemed. All the other girls liked her too; nobody had a bad word to say about her.

This was not going to be an easy case for Clarke, but Kevin had a lot of confidence in him. He had a proven track record, which was unusual at only twenty-nine years old. He had masterminded the capture of a drugs ring, and also been instrumental in getting justice and a new life for the vulnerable girls who had been used and abused by the gang.

He had also tracked down and captured the kidnapper of the young son of a wealthy Arabian businessman. The three year old child had been traumatised, but Alan's calm and kindly manner had won him over, and nobody could have been more grateful than the child's parents when he was returned home safely and unharmed. Clarke had chased down the kidnapper and arrested him, and his bravery when the thug was wielding a knife at him had been truly inspirational. He had managed to get him to drop the knife, and the thug was now safely incarcerated.

With only a year left until he retired, Kevin was happy to leave the physical part of the job to younger men. He would be retiring with a healthy pension and a wealth of memories, some good and some bad. He could now indulge his hobby of playing golf, and take more cruises and see the world.

He had spent years putting the job before anything else, and it had almost cost him his marriage. Soon it was going to be Kevin and Naomi's time. His long-suffering wife had put up with many disappointments over the years; cancelled events and holidays, lonely anniversary and birthday evenings, but not any more.

"A penny for your thoughts?"

She was standing there with the coffee pot in her hand, and he held out his cup.

"Yes please, darling, I was just thinking how nice it would be to go on a world cruise after I leave."

Chapter Seven

Ruth and Gerald Ryder had been living in Whitstable for just two months. Both in their early fifties and now living their dream of escaping from the rat race of London, and jobs that involved sitting in an office and looking out onto nothing but greyness. It had been lovely leaving behind crowded tube trains, and people always in a hurry.

They had embraced the clean fresh air of Whitstable, the friendliness of the local folk, the peaceful harbour, and the diverse shops along the main street. They were indulging their dream to be self employed, having bought a three storey Victorian house in a side street, which they intended to convert into a bed and breakfast business.

It nestled between many other terraced buildings in the narrow street, all deceptively larger than they appeared from the outside. Most of these houses belonged to people who lived in London, and were either used as a holiday home, or let out to others who could enjoy a week away from the hustle and bustle of the city.

Whitstable was a popular holiday destination, as it was the nearest coastal town from London and most of the journey could be covered by motorway. During the summer the Oyster Festival took place and, over that weekend, the town was so full of visitors it came to a standstill, with streets closed and all the car parks full.

Pavement artists abounded there and could be seen at work, which was fascinating to onlookers. Local shops stocked memorabilia of times past, and the local Tudor Restaurant boasted of having had the late Peter Cushing as a regular customer for many years.

Ruth still felt young and energetic, and moving to the coast had made her more conscious about keeping fit. She was naturally slim, and kept herself fit by doing a lot of walking, and then she decided to join a yoga class. The ladies of Whitstable were very friendly, and she was invited to join other clubs.

She had her hair done at the local salon. Like her daughter Zoe, it was naturally curly, and she made sure that her highlights were touched up whenever they needed it. She always wanted to look her best.

They had made enough money from the sale of their house in Wimbledon to buy this one, and then they also had some money left over to spend on modernising and redecorating it. Plans had recently been submitted to the council for their intended alterations, and they already had a builder lined up to do the work when they got the go ahead.

Gerald had joined the local golf club, and he had also taken up fishing. He seemed to like sitting for ages waiting to get a bite. Although this wouldn't have suited Ruth, he obviously found it peaceful after all the years spent in London. He had promised himself, when the house project was finished, if there was enough money left over, he would get himself a little boat with an outboard motor, and then he could explore the meandering river Stour, which flowed through many picturesque places.

Their move had taken place just two weeks before Adam was born. It wasn't planned to be then, but thanks to the chain being broken several times, it had dragged on until completion. They had dashed back to Dulwich to see him, and the pride they felt was totally overwhelming.

Ruth was pleased that Alan had taken some time off to support Zoe after the birth. If he hadn't, no matter how difficult it was, Ruth had decided she would step in. After a couple of weeks, Alan had brought Zoe and Adam down for the day, but they had to return home that same evening. Ruth had been hoping they could all get together some time soon, as she didn't want to miss her grandson growing up. They all seemed to have such busy lives right now.

They did telephone each other regularly, but it wasn't the same as being together. Zoe's sister Julie and her husband lived in Australia, they had emigrated a few years previously, and Ruth had found that quite a wrench, contenting herself with speaking to them on Skype and making the occasional visit. At least Zoe and Alan were here in England, so she felt they must make the time to get together.

She felt the buzz of her mobile in her pocket, and when she lifted it out Zoe's name flashed up on her screen.

"Hello darling, how are you, and how is Adam?"

"Fine Mum, it's all good. I was wondering if you and Dad would like us to come and stay for maybe a couple of weeks or longer?"

"You know we would. Is it just you and Adam?" she asked, puzzled.

Zoe laughed. "Do you honestly think Alan would be parted from Adam for that long? No, I meant all of us."

Ruth felt really happy at the prospect. She didn't need to ask Gerald, she knew he would love having them to stay as much as her.

"Well, there is a complete unit you can have to yourselves at the top of the house, if you want some space. Up there is a bedroom and en suite, a lounge, and even a small kitchen, but of course we hope you will eat with us."

"It sounds absolutely perfect, Mum. I think I remember you showing us when we came down for the day. Alan has been asked to cover a case in Herne Bay, and he will be working from Canterbury police station. It may take a few weeks, and he will have Wendy working alongside him as well."

"Oh yes, of course, the girl on the beach. It shook everyone, as nothing like that has ever happened here before. Have they got any suspects?"

"Now, Mum, you know that Alan is sworn to secrecy. I would never ask him. We will know soon enough when he solves the murder."

"It has certainly upset people. The local news has been full of it. Does Wendy want to stay here as well? We can find room for her."

"That is very kind of you, Mum, but evidently she has been told she will be staying at the Marine Hotel."

"Wow, that lovely one along Tankerton seafront. She will be spoiled there."

"And she can have her own space. I am glad you have put us right up the top, Mum, then you won't hear Adam fussing in the evening."

"Don't be silly dear, we can take it in turns to hold him. You are certainly not going to shut yourself up there with him!" said Ruth very firmly, and Zoe felt a warm feeling steal over her. Even at the age of twenty-six, her mum still made everything feel right. Alan could concentrate on his case, and Zoe and Ruth could spend some quality time together.

"Thanks, Mum, you are a star!" she said warmly. Now I can tell Alan.

Alan was busily reading up about Sadie Morton Brown, and the case fourteen years ago. So when Zoe rang his mobile, and said her mum and dad would love to have them to stay, and they could even have their own little separate area at the top of the house, he felt pleased. Wendy was perfectly happy to accompany him. A change of scenery, and a new case to solve was the sort of challenge she really liked.

He telephoned through to Chief Superintendent Kevin Watts on his private number, and reiterated his willingness to take on the case with the help of Wendy. Kevin beamed at the other end of the line. This was good news.

"Great, Clarke. So how soon can you and your partner get yourselves down to Herne Bay to do the interviewing?"

"Today, right away, sir. My wife is packing as we speak."

"Well, today you must report to Canterbury Police station. As it is Saturday, there will only be skeleton staff and I think they close at four o'clock. There will be a team waiting for you tomorrow morning, so you need to fill them in on your movements. We need this murder inquiry wrapped up as quickly as possible, as we can't afford for this nice little seaside town to have a stigma attached to it. People want to come on holiday with complete confidence in knowing that they and their children are safe."

"Of course, I fully understand that, sir."

"Oh, by the way Clarke, it will probably help you quite a bit to familiarise yourself with the Morton Brown family, and particularly Sadie, before you start doing the interviews."

"Yes sir, I have been doing that, and she is a fascinating character."

"Good, I will let Canterbury know, and leave you to get yourself going now."

Kevin smiled to himself when he came off the telephone. He really felt confident that he had chosen the right person to take on this job. Young Clarke was already getting his teeth into it!

Chapter Eight

"Granma, I need to pick up a flight right now. My folks want me back home."

Billy's voice sounded desperate, he just knew that the police would be round soon, and it definitely wasn't looking good for him. What a fool he had been to give Dee a drag on his cigarette. If only he had known it would knock her out. It was supposed to do the opposite!

Then there was Janet; not only pregnant, but also dead on the beach at the same time that he was there. He had always enjoyed visiting his rich grandparents here, but right now he couldn't wait to leave England.

Isabel glanced over at him. Her grandson looked uncannily like his mother Sadie; the same dark eyes, and air of mystery, although his hair was a lighter shade of brown, more the colour of his father's. Both Philip and herself had tried to make it up to him that he had been adopted.

Nobody had been more shocked than herself and Philip to find out that Sadie had been married before, and had a son. She had not confided in them or Nathan, maybe she was ashamed that she couldn't cope with him, because that would have been the reason she had him adopted. Finding herself left to bring up a child after the divorce might have been just too much for her, so she had tried to give him a better life.

They had met Ricky, he had been in England when Sadie met her tragic death in a street accident. To them he seemed to be a nice young man, so they had no idea why the marriage had failed, and Ricky didn't speak about it. Indeed, he had suffered his own heartbreak when his first wife had also been killed in a car crash, and he was left to bring up three young daughters alone.

But it hadn't stopped him from seeking out his son, and trying to guide him in the right direction in life. It was clear, as soon as you met Billy, that he had a huge hang-up about losing his mother and father, and being adopted.

They made excuses for Billy's arrogance, and, with them, he did show a human side. Philip had suggested that they pay for him to finish his education in England, because he had a history of dropping out of college. And maybe if he was given another chance like Nathan had, he might make something of himself in life. But right now fear registered in his eyes, and Isabel didn't want to think badly of him. Having lost both her young son and her daughter made her grandchildren even more precious to her. She believed that with a bit of support from them, Billy would grow out of this awkward phase.

When they had heard that their precious Dee was in hospital, having been found unconscious on the beach yesterday, the inclination of both Philip and Isabel was to drop everything and head straight to the hospital. But Nathan had discouraged them saying that Dee was OK and she was sleeping.

He reassured them that the doctors had found nothing physically wrong with her, and she would be home tomorrow, which meant they could stick to the original arrangements and come round with Billy to visit her. But now Billy wanted to go back to the States, and very quickly, too.

Whatever had happened, Isabel knew for sure that Dee would not have done anything to poor Janet. She was a sweet and affectionate girl. Her nature was uncomplicated; what you saw was exactly what you got with Dee, she had no hidden agenda, and she didn't possess a mean bone in her body.

Rumours were circulating wildly, suggesting that Janet had teased Dee about her mother's past, but even that wouldn't have provoked her to do something violent. She was just not made that way. They needed to get her back home quickly, and then Philip would make absolutely sure there was no more bullying towards Dee at school.

As for Billy, he didn't spend enough time with them to properly work him out, and still waters did run deep. But Isabel still felt that, no matter what had happened, he would have to stay and face the music. There was going to be no quick way out for him.

"We can't send you back, Billy, you must realise that. Your girlfriend is dead, and your sister was found unconscious on the beach, we all need to know exactly what happened," said Isabel.

"I hope you are not accusing me!" said Billy, indignantly.

"We just think you should care a little about what has happened, and not run off as soon as things become tough," said Philip, very pointedly. "Your family here need you."

Billy could see that he was caught like a rat in a trap. He had no money of his own to buy a plane ticket, and he realised that both of his grandparents were not budging. He didn't want to be arrested and thrown into jail, but there was so much evidence against him, what chance did he stand? His voice became pleading.

"I really have no idea how Janet died, but it was nothing to do with me. We had words, and then she took off in a huff and I never saw her again."

"We were not thinking that at all, and if you explain it to the police, it will clear you from even being a suspect. Who knows, Janet might have actually died accidentally, you can't believe half of what is printed in the newspapers," said Philip reflectively.

Billy did not like the mention of the cops. He had been in trouble with the law in America. When he became bored, he decided to add a bit of excitement to his life, so he stole a couple of cars and went joyriding. His father had managed to get him put on probation, and made sure he behaved himself after that.

Billy could still remember how Jill had wept when she found out what he had done. He knew he was a disappointment to them, but they didn't understand how he felt abandoned by his real mother, and it had made him feel worthless.

Ricky had tried to explain that Sadie had done it for Billy's own good, as she couldn't cope with him as a single mother, and that he should be grateful to Jill and Simon for giving him a new life. But Billy couldn't feel at all grateful, because he had grown up in poverty, he completely disregarded the love that they had always showered over him. When he finally discovered that he had rich grandparents, that had been a good day for him.

He did have a certain respect for his father; because he was an FBI man, he had managed to make the authorities aware that he would keep him in line, so his position had been handy. So Billy had made a bit of an effort as he realised he could no longer go joyriding in other people's cars.

His grandfather had added an incentive to him pursuing his studies by suggesting that if he worked properly, and didn't waste the opportunity, maybe he would pay for him to continue his education in England.

He wasn't impressed to find out that he had a younger sister. Dee was quiet, unlike the image he had of her flamboyant mother. He felt jealousy towards her. After all, Sadie had not had her adopted, and Dee had grown up in the midst of a wealthy family, and wanted for nothing. By all accounts it seemed that Dee and Sadie had enjoyed a close relationship. She now called Nathan 'Dad,' and he had adopted her by changing her name to Edwards. If the rumours were true, her father was really the now deceased footballer Danny Foster. It was before Billy's time, but evidently he had been known as 'The Golden Boy' of English football.

"Waal, of course I care," he drawled. "It's been such a huge shock. Have you told my father?"

"Not yet. Nothing much to tell," said Philip.

There was a pregnant pause, which was soon broken by the sound of the buzzer, which meant there was someone at the gate waiting to be let in. Billy's heart lurched, this was it!

Alan had to drop off Zoe and Adam at the Whitstable house with a promise to help her unpack later, as he had to report to Canterbury Police Station that afternoon. Kevin had told him there would only be minimum staff there. Wendy was in the car, and he drove round to the Marine Hotel so she could check in and leave her luggage in her room.

Her bedroom was very attractive, and there was a small sitting room attached with a large TV, and a very comfortable sofa. The en suite had a bath and a shower, and the view of the grass area with the beach in the background caught her attention immediately.

People could be seen walking along the grass; families with dogs and children on bicycles, all enjoying the spring sunshine.

Opposite the hotel, overlooking the beach, was an ice cream booth, and because it was Saturday, the queue was very long, but nobody seemed to mind. Who wanted to rush anywhere with the afternoon sun beaming down, anyway?

Alan drove along the seafront, and then picked up the road into Canterbury, negotiating his way through the traffic. His satnav had brought him this way, and even the main through road was in no way as busy as any of the roads around Dulwich. The A205 had always been full of traffic no matter what time of the day he drove along it.

They arrived at the station at three o'clock, which gave them an hour before it closed at four. Enough time for them to familiarise themselves with the case. The station was set on the corner of the main high street in Canterbury, with gates leading to a car park at the back, which opened as soon as they announced themselves.

They were welcomed into the station by Constable Gary Hill, a man in his early thirties with brown hair and an earnest looking face. He had a rather bored looking WPC standing next to him, who was introduced as Mandy. She was about the same age as Wendy, and short and stocky with fair hair.

"As you can see by all the empty spaces, it's just us this afternoon. We had more officers on duty this morning, but we are due to close in an hour. However, we thought it important to let you know exactly how far we have got with this case," said Gary.

"Of course, and we know you probably want to head off and enjoy the rest of the weekend, so thank you for being here to see us," said Alan, which elicited a smile from the deadpan face of Mandy.

Gary explained that interviews with the students had taken place at the school earlier that morning, and all fingerprints had now been taken. This was because Dee had been dragged up the beach by an unknown person. Unfortunately, due to being in the water, there were no fingerprints on the body of the murdered girl.

Dee had been interviewed in hospital the evening before, but didn't appear to remember how she had ended up on the beach, and her half-brother Billy had not yet been interviewed. He was Janet's on/off boyfriend. Tests had shown that the deceased victim, Janet, had been about six weeks pregnant.

He also explained that Janet didn't appear to be that popular with the other girls, and she had preyed on Dee, and taunted her about her mother's past.

"Well, that makes it a lot harder to find the culprit, if she was disliked. But it sounds like the first person we need to interview is Billy. We need to find out if he knew that she was pregnant."

"You can leave it until Monday if you prefer, sir."

"Absolutely not, there is no time like the present!"

Wendy said nothing, she knew that Alan was champing at the bit right now. Even though they had only just arrived, and her hotel looked inviting, settling in would have to wait, because once Alan got his teeth into something, there was no stopping him.

"What about Zoe?" she reminded him.

"Oh, I can soon fix that," said Alan confidently, feeling in his pocket for his mobile, then continuing: "In the meantime, can you give us the names and addresses of all the people we need to interview?"

"Here we are, sir," said Gary, holding out a sheaf of papers which Wendy took from him, whilst Alan was engrossed in his mobile, and had turned the other way.

Alan rang Zoe, and it was exactly as he had thought. She didn't want to waste a minute of the beautiful sunshine, so she had gone out for a walk with Adam and his proud new grandma. She told him they were strolling along the promenade, and Adam was fast asleep. Zoe said she was quite happy that he would not be back for over an hour, because they had walked along as far as Tankerton, and it would easily take an hour or more to get back.

Alan was very impressed with the home of Philip and Isabel Morton Brown. Although it was all contained on one floor, it could hardly be called a bungalow. It nestled among a tree-lined area, the back garden had panoramic views of the sea, whilst the front of the building overlooked the fields of a local farm. There was a carpet of bluebells in the front garden, and pink and white blossoms adorned the trees.

The country lane was too narrow for parking and Alan noted that, to be able to drive inside, they would need to press the buzzer and announce themselves, then the rustic wooden gates would open.

He dutifully pressed the buzzer, then a man's voice, which he guessed to be that of Philip Morton Brown, spoke. "Yes, who is it?"

"Good afternoon, I am Detective Chief Inspector Alan Clarke, and I have my partner WPC Wendy Stuart with me. We would like to speak to Billy Hopkins if that is possible please."

"You best come in then."

Philip wasn't sure whether he felt relieved or not. They were going round to Nathan's and Lydia's house, and this would make them late, but at least the dreaded interview would then be over and done with.

"Isabel, can you send Nathan a text to explain we will be a little late, whilst I let the police in," he said.

"Of course, and Billy, just tell the truth and then everything will be fine," said Isabel patting her grandson's shoulder gently.

Alan took in the opulence of this luxury home as soon as they parked in the paved area. There was enough room for about six cars and a double garage, which was flanked on either side by young trees. The winding path stretched from the end of the paved area up to the front door, with grass areas each side. All along the edges were shrubs, which were neatly shaped and very well tended. A wooden bench was set outside the front door, with a tub of colourful flowers next to it. And instead of flower beds, there were tiny pieces of grey slate, which looked really classy.

When they reached the front door, it was opened by an elderly man, probably in his early seventies, but still looking very distinguished, with greyish white hair, and a slim and tall frame. He was wearing oatmeal coloured trousers with a short sleeved cream shirt, which was obviously very good quality. He shook Alan's hand.

"Good afternoon DCI Clarke, I am Philip Morton Brown."

"Good afternoon, Mr Morton Brown, this is my assistant WPC Wendy Stuart."

Philip smiled and shook her hand, and Wendy noted that he had a kind face, and, in spite of his wealth, no sign of arrogance. They were shown along the hall, which had a cream carpet with very thick pile, and she noticed there were various family photographs on the wall.

In pride of place was a large sized photograph of a young girl with beautiful long black hair. But her most striking feature was her eyes; like black coals, dark, smouldering and sultry. Wendy guessed this must have been Sadie.

Next to it was a photograph of a young boy, maybe about three or four years old, she guessed this must have been her brother Jeremy, who had tragically drowned. What an unlucky family they were.

There was also a photograph of Sadie on her wedding day with Nathan, and what a handsome couple they made. Sadie was smiling, and flushed with happiness, and in that photograph, her eyes looked completely different, they were warm and friendly. The little girl nestling into the side of her had to be Dee at about five years old. Wendy couldn't help feeling such empathy for these parents who had lost so much, and now it looked like tragedy had struck their family again.

They were shown into a room which was obviously a library, bookcases filled the walls, and at the far end was a desk with a swivel chair and a home computer. At the side there were two sofas opposite one another, from which a lady and a young man rose to greet them. The lady was also elderly, but her face still showed signs of beauty, with her long dark hair swept elegantly on top of her head, and her frame was still slim. She wore a simple white skirt with a pale blue blouse, and she moved very gracefully across the room to greet them.

"Good afternoon. I am Isabel, and this is our grandson Billy."

Alan took in the scene, noting that both Isabel and Philip, although middle class, were very polite and respectful towards him. They didn't make him feel as though he was wasting their time, which made him warm towards them. Sometimes in the past, people

71

who had money felt themselves to be really special but they still had to be treated the same as anyone else.

As he studied Billy, he noted his body language was very nervous, but it didn't stop him from being arrogant, as if none of it was anything to do with him.

"Sir, I am Billy, on vacation right now, and we are due to pay a visit to Nathan and Lydia, and my sister Dee."

"It's OK Billy," Isabel reminded him. "I sent a text to say we would be a little late. How can we help you DCI Clarke?" She met Alan's glance unflinchingly.

"We just wanted to ask Billy a few questions about yesterday."

Isabel smiled. "Would you like a cup of tea?"

"What a good idea, many thanks, milk and one sugar for both of us," said Wendy quickly, knowing that Alan could concentrate better on Billy with less people around. She took out her notebook and pen, ready to start.

"Do sit down and make yourselves comfortable," said Philip hospitably. He sat next to Billy, who he could see was a bit uptight, hoping his presence might make him feel less nervous. Alan noted that Billy had the same unfathomable look in his dark eyes as Sadie in the large photograph, although his hair colouring was lighter; it was mid brown.

Alan smiled pleasantly at Billy, noticing there was no smile back.

"Billy, can you tell me about your movements yesterday afternoon?"

Billy was wondering if there was something he could say which didn't link him to the beach. He had no scruples about lying if it got him off the hook. But then he had told Isabel he was going to meet Janet, and also Dee was bound to have told them too that she saw him. Whether she would have mentioned that she had a puff of his cigarette, he couldn't be sure, or even whether she had realised she had a puff of pot. He tried to play it cool.

"In the afternoon I went down to the shore to meet Janet. I had just got in for my vacation that morning. But we only spent a very short time together before she went off. Then I saw my sister Dee. She didn't stop either, so I came home."

"Was Janet your girlfriend?"

72

"Not a serious one, just when I came over on vacation."

Alan considered his words, it somehow didn't make sense.

"So you saw your sister and your girlfriend on the beach, but neither of them spent any time with you. Had you had an argument with either of them?"

Billy's eyes were glittering strangely with suppressed rage. He knew better than to lose his temper now, especially with his granddad sitting right next to him.

"Janet was in a mood. I came here for a vacation, not to have her shout at me."

Alan really didn't like this cocky young man, he was so self-centred, so he made his next words strong.

"Am I right in thinking that Janet shouted at you because she told you she was pregnant, and you were not prepared to stand by her?"

Isabel entered the room at that moment with a tray of tea and biscuits, hearing every word.

"Oh no, Billy," she said sorrowfully, as she set the tray on the table, and the look of dismay on Philip's face matched hers. Could this really be true?

The conversation stopped whilst Isabel handed out tea and biscuits to everyone, and Billy tried to think quickly how he could get out of this. This nosy cop was making sure they thought the worst of him, and that would not help him in the future. Inside he was uttering every single expletive that he could think of, but this man could easily make his grandpa think twice about paying for his schooling, and allowing him to stay in England next year.

"Yea, she said she was pregnant, but how did I know it was mine? When I went back home she was free to date anyone."

His cold manner startled Alan. He didn't appear to have any emotion, nor had he expressed any regret about her death. He seemed to have no respect for the poor girl, who he more than likely had made pregnant.

"We can soon check if the baby was yours, you know, so you need to be straight with me. Did you have a sexual relationship with Janet?"

Billy was used to wriggling out of situations by using his good looks and charm, and it was only then that the coldness left his eyes.

d

Replaced by a smile, and a look of sincerity. He found it always worked with women, but this nosy cop had a steely determined look in his eyes, and he wasn't sure it would work with him. At that moment, Billy's arrogance left him, he was no longer very sure of himself. But being so aware of his grandparents listening to everything, he had to make it sound good.

"Yes sir, I did, but we were not dating as such. When I went home, I never asked her if she was seeing someone else." Turning to his grandmother, and allowing his eyes to soften, he added, "Of course, if the baby had turned out to be mine, I would have stood by Janet, and supported her in any way that I possibly could."

To Isabel that statement appeared to have been spoken with absolute sincerity. It resonated with her that sometimes people misjudged Billy. Of course he would have stood by his girlfriend. She really wanted to believe that about him. Both she and Philip had tried so hard to make him feel wanted, because he bore the scars of a rejected child. If he had not stood by Janet, his own child would have grown up feeling the same.

Billy knew those words sounded really good, especially as he didn't have a single dime in the world. He had never even been able to save any pocket money he had been given. If Janet had been pregnant by him, he would have had to go to Philip and Isabel, cap in hand, and ask them to give her some sort of settlement or allowance. After all, they did have more money than they knew what to do with.

His mind wandered a little, realising that he didn't even know if they had made any provision for him in their wills. They were both knocking on a bit now, they wouldn't live forever. But he scowled to himself when he realised that they had more than likely left it all to Dee, and maybe even to the pretender Jack, who called himself Dee's brother, but was in no way blood related to her grandparents, yet they treated him as if he was family too.

Alan didn't believe a word that Billy was saying. There was nothing sincere about him at all. One minute he was trying to dodge out of it, and then the next he was pretending he would have supported the girl. No doubt he would have hot-footed it back to the States, but that would have hurt him financially, to be away for any length of time from his wealthy grandparents. He didn't strike Alan as being a loving grandson. He had noticed him trying to soft soap his grandmother, and it looked like it had worked. But, he reminded himself, just because he disliked a suspect, that did not necessarily mean they were guilty, and there were quite a few more people to interview. There was something else he wanted to clear up.

"When you saw your sister Dee, how did she look? Were you surprised to hear that she had collapsed on the beach, presumably after you left her?"

Billy licked his dry lips whilst he contemplated how much he could actually tell him without landing himself in even more trouble. Maybe Dee had told them he had given her a drag on a cigarette, but he was pretty sure she didn't realise he was smoking dope, or she would never have touched it. He felt he could afford to be economical with the truth.

"She was very stressed when I saw her, so I offered her a drag on my cigarette. It seemed to calm her. She did not tell me why she was upset. We do not confide in each other, and I did not ask. I left her sitting on the beach."

"You didn't ask?" persisted Alan.

"I did not. Like I said, we do not confide in each other."

"I think Dee may have been stressed because she was near to the glen, and the headland," explained Isabel. "She doesn't usually walk that way because she saw her nanny fall over the cliff and die at the headland some years ago. She had counselling at the time, but she usually stays near to the pier and the bandstand when she takes walks."

"I see, so what would have been her reason for going that way yesterday?"

"I have no idea, but I am sure she will be able to tell you herself."

"Yes, that is fine. We will talk to her later, so we won't take up any more of your time."

"We are off to see her ourselves this afternoon, so we best get ready," said Philip.

Alan and Wendy got up to go, but then Alan remembered something. Billy wouldn't like this at all, but tough!

"Oh yes, Billy, I forgot to mention this before; could you please report to Canterbury police station on Monday to have your fingerprints taken."

"Why?" demanded Billy, remembering he had probably left his prints all over that call box, and the cops would be all over it.

"Well, just about every girl in Dee's class has had theirs taken, so we didn't want to leave you out," said Alan sarcastically. No way was he going to tell him anything. This little upstart thought he could outsmart him but he couldn't.

"OK," he said sullenly.

"If you present yourself about ten o'clock at the desk, it will all be done very quickly," Alan said smoothly.

"We can run you over," said Isabel, trying to make the situation better. Alan guessed they would do that for a quiet life, although he wondered what was wrong with a twenty-year-old getting the number seven bus into Canterbury; it virtually passed the door. They definitely did spoil him.

With the interview now over, Isabel thanked them for coming and showed them out.

Chapter Nine

Alan was finding it quite a relief that he could get on with his job without disrupting his family life too much, so soon after Adam's birth. Zoe had always known the score; his job was a demanding one, and sometimes he had to work unsociable hours including weekends. And since his son was born, he was even more aware of it.

Zoe had a year of maternity leave, so she would eventually return to work, and then they would have to look at getting some extra help, either from a nanny or by sending Adam to a nursery, so the time that she spent with Adam now whilst he was so young, was very precious to her.

Coming to Whitstable and staying with her parents had been a great idea. Ruth could hardly bear to put her grandson down, and he was being spoiled, but both Alan and Zoe were quite relaxed about it, because it was lovely to see the bond being cemented between them. Gerald, too, was a proud granddad, and on Sunday they asked Alan if he minded if they walked him around to the house of one of their friends, as they wanted to show him off.

"Of course I don't mind," said Alan.

"You mean to tell me you are not going fishing?" said Ruth, surprised.

"I can do that any time," interjected Gerald, tickling Adam under the chin.

"Of course, we will miss you, but if you are doing more

interviews today, it's no problem," said Zoe smiling. She knew him so well. Once he started on a case, he would really get stuck in, no matter what day of the week it was.

Alan hugged her gratefully. His wife was the best, he was so lucky!

"Yes, I need to press on, and I am so glad your parents are having some quality time with Adam."

He could not help thinking wistfully about his own parents, taken too soon, after the aircraft carrying them back from a holiday in New Zealand, only last year, had crashed with no survivors. It had been such a tragedy, and although his parents had been to their wedding, they had never known that Zoe was carrying their grandchild. Alan had been devastated, and his way of coping had been to bury himself in work, so when Zoe had told him about her pregnancy, he had found concentrating on her had helped with his grief. Her strength and support towards him had got him through. He felt without her he would not have coped. It still hurt him, but having Adam to focus on as well as a busy working life really did help.

Zoe knew what he was thinking, and her heart went out to him, so she squeezed his hand gently. No words were needed, they both knew what that meant. To the rest of the world Alan appeared to be a tough and strong man, he had to be for the job he did, but she knew that inside he was still hurting.

Alan brought his mind back to the task in hand. Today he wanted to interview Dee. He was finding the Morton Brown family very interesting, and he wondered whether Dee had the same mystery about her that Sadie had possessed.

Certainly Billy seemed to have the same traits as his mother. Alan had read up a lot about Sadie Morton Brown. When she was incarcerated another side to her complex character had emerged. She had lost her coldness and apparent lack of emotion. She had been a model prisoner, and declared she had found God. Many prisoners did the same in an effort to get out as soon as they could, but then some went back to their criminal ways again.

Sadie had been discharged after four years. It was believed that she was no danger to society, and although she was still suffering from a mental condition, she was given medication to help her to cope with it. And it seemed like she had, as she reconciled with her mother after years of arguing, and had taken her duty of being a good mother to Dee very seriously.

Nobody would ever know for sure if she had killed Danny Foster. It could have been a crime of passion because he rejected her and his child, as the verdict had been an open one. He couldn't swim, so he may have drowned, as he was well over the limit at the time. Or he may have taken his own life because he had been dropped by the team. Football always came before everything in his life.

Sadie had always protested her innocence, but that was not reliable because most prisoners said that. She was certainly an intriguing character, and her untimely death somehow made her seem like a tragic character, as did the family that she had left behind.

His mobile rang, and he answered it quickly as Wendy's name flashed up.

"Good morning, sir, we have an interview with Dee Edwards at eleven o'clock. She returned home from hospital yesterday afternoon."

"Oh, that is great, Wendy. I will get ready and come and pick you up. How is your room?"

"Lovely sir, and the food," she said warmly. "I could stay here forever!"

"Couldn't we both! Zoe is loving it here. I have yet to explore Whitstable and the surrounding area."

Dee was expecting to hear soon that she would be interviewed again. The interview in the hospital had only been a preliminary one. Having had a restful day at home on Saturday, she was feeling much better. Her grandparents and Billy had come round on Saturday afternoon, and for once Billy didn't seem totally full of his own self importance. He had even asked how she was feeling now, and if she could remember seeing him on the beach. She did recall it now, and the strange smelling cigarette that she had taken a puff of, but after that her memory became hazy.

Dee was naïve, and until then, had never tried to smoke a

cigarette. Nobody with any sense would do it in these enlightened times. Her mother had never smoked, and Nathan and Lydia had warned her of the perils. Nathan had been honest, he said years ago he had tried it, but realised how bad it was for him, so had given up.

She didn't want to end up with lung disease and a shortened life, so she felt quite horrified with herself that she had even tried it, and although she knew very little about smoking, instinct told her it wasn't just an ordinary cigarette. Whatever would her parents, and gran and granddad, think of her?

Billy took the opportunity to enlighten her when Dee slipped into the kitchen to get a glass of water.

"Dee, I think the cops will want to speak to you soon. I told them you had a drag on my cigarette, but I didn't tell 'em it was weed," he whispered guiltily, and Dee swung round from the sink, feeling horrified.

"OMG. I didn't know that!"

"And you mustn't tell anyone. We will be in deep trouble."

Dee knew this was true, and she wished she hadn't taken that puff. It hadn't done her any good, and might even have been the cause of her blackout. Whatever was Billy doing with his life to smoke this stuff? She spoke her mind.

"I won't give it away, Billy, but for goodness sake, why do you do it?"

"It makes me feel good!" said Billy, obstinately.

"Well it didn't do me any good; it made me faint! Wherever did you get it from?"

"I can't tell you that. But sis, I will try and kick the habit, so nobody needs to know."

Dee always wanted to think the best of everyone, so his reply was a relief. If Billy made an effort to stop, then there was no harm done. She would be honest with the police, but chances are they wouldn't ask what she had been smoking.

"OK, as long as you ditch it!"

She smiled at him, and Billy knew then he had fooled her. He had no intention of giving up his recreational drug, but Dee wasn't worldly-wise, and she believed him. Part of him scorned her naivety. Her character was nothing like their feisty mother had been. He felt he was probably more like Sadie, so who did Dee take after?

Although it wasn't what she wanted, Dee had been reassured by Philip and Nathan that when she returned to school on Monday there would be no more bullying. Now that the head had been made aware of it, a special assembly had taken place before they had all been interviewed, and the girls were told that if the bullying continued, the pupils who were doing it would be immediately expelled.

Dee had already felt the other girls were led on by Janet. None of them had the guts to stand alone. They were just like sheep basically, so nobody would dare to do it. As always, she had the support of Beth, so her life at school would be less tumultuous.

But she had also guessed that her family would intervene just to hammer the point home, and in her heart she couldn't be angry with them, because knowing how much they cared about her welfare gave her a warm glow inside. She now felt a renewed strength inside herself, and she vowed to fight back. Maybe she should have done this before instead of letting Janet see just how upset she was. It had taken the sad death of Janet to make her realise that she must stand up to bullies.

Today the sun continued to shine, and it looked like summer had arrived early, so she dressed herself in white shorts and a peach coloured tee shirt, which accentuated her light golden tan and her very dark eyes. Dee knew she looked like her mother at the same age, she had seen the photograph that had pride of place in her grand arents' hall, and she felt proud to be like her, because everyone had considered her mother to be very beautiful.

Lydia interrupted her reverie to enquire if she felt OK, and would she like some breakfast?

"Yes please. I will come down in a minute. I can make it myself."

"I have made a saucepan full of porridge if you fancy it."

"Why not."

Dee smiled to herself, guessing that Lydia was trying to encourage them all to eat more healthily. She often watched programmes about good diets, and it certainly worked for her, as she had a nice trim figure. Dee was still at the age where she could eat anything and not put on weight.

Recently Nathan had been for a routine check at the doctor's and had been told if he changed his diet a little, he wouldn't need to take any medication to lower his cholesterol, and apparently starting the day off with a bowl of porridge was a step in the right direction. Sunday breakfast was usually eggs and bacon, so it was no surprise that Jack and Nathan seemed less than impressed with the idea of porridge.

When she came downstairs and into the kitchen, Jack was sitting there eating his porridge, and then Nathan joined them.

"Can I have a bacon sandwich after?" Jack asked.

"Whatever is this gruel?" joked Nathan, as he sat down.

"Porridge is recommended to lower cholesterol," said Lydia defensively, putting porridge into three bowls, and then sitting down to eat some herself.

Dee smiled, this felt a bit like Goldilocks and the three bears. Poor Lydia, she was doing her best.

"It's very nice,"she said, spooning some into her mouth.

"I will do some bacon sandwiches as well," said Lydia, realising they were not quite ready for a change, so she would have to compromise. She smiled at them all dutifully eating, and ignored the faces that Jack was pulling.

The telephone rang and Nathan went to answer it. He returned quickly, with the phone in his hand.

"The police would like to come round and interview you this morning, Dee. Do you feel up to it?"

"Of course, Daddy, it's fine," she reassured him.

A time of eleven o'clock was set, and this time Dee felt really calm. She had been expecting it, although she wasn't sure how much use she would be to them. She still couldn't remember much about fainting on the beach, nor could she remember seeing Janet there, although she did think she had seen her on the way there. Maybe chatting about it to the police would help her to remember more. Her nature was a placid one; she never looked for trouble, and in spite of her lapse of memory, she was certain that Janet's death had nothing to do with her.

After breakfast she helped Lydia to load their plates into the dishwasher, and then sat in the conservatory, looking over towards the sea. It was lapping very gently up the beach, and with the sun reflecting on it, gave off a most beautiful greenish blue hue. Watching the waves slowly covering the beach had a calming effect on her.

Dee, herself, wanted to know why her mind was blank after reaching the beach. She felt angry with herself for fainting. She had always been stoic. Her short life so far had always been punctuated by dramas, and with the help of Maria Firth, her private psychologist from Harley Street, she had risen above it, and found an inner strength to carry on.

That was until Janet started taunting her about her mother's past. If she had said nasty things about Dee, she would have laughed it off, but the memory of her mother was so preciously locked away inside her heart, she could not bear anyone to tarnish it. With what she had gone through, most sixteen year olds would have fallen apart, but underneath her calm and naturally happy exterior lay a resilience that few girls of her own age would possess.

Now that all her fears and insecurities had once again been laid bare, she could talk it through with Maria, who would help her as she had done before. She was such an easy woman to talk to; pouring out her grief, even shedding a few tears in the past, had really helped her. Being such a young girl, and seeing her nanny die in front of her, and then losing her much loved mother afterwards, had been overwhelming.

Nathan and her grandparents had tried so hard to act normally in front of her but, being such a sensitive girl, she could not fail to see the grief in their eyes. Then gradually normality had been resumed when Lydia had come to live with them.

She heard the doorbell go. Nathan said he would deal with it, so she stood up and tuned towards the door, waiting for it to open. When it did, it was to admit a man in plain clothes, accompanied by a young lady, also in plain clothes. To Dee, they didn't look that formidable.

Alan was well versed in appraising the characters of witnesses. It was very necessary in this job not to be taken in by people, but he knew he also had to be careful about prejudging people as well. Some characters could be really dislikeable, but that didn't mean that they were guilty. Having read about what an extrovert character Sadie had been, he was interested to see if her daughter possessed any of Sadie's traits.

Nathan introduced them to her, whilst explaining that Dee was now feeling better after her stay in hospital over night, and some restful time at home afterwards. Alan noted the concerned look in his eyes when he spoke to Dee, and how she smiled back at him, and patted his hand when she spoke. It was clear that they were very close.

"Yes, I am fine now, Dad."

He couldn't miss Nathan's protectiveness towards her. He also noticed how politely she stood to greet him; unlike Billy, who had been slouching on the sofa the previous day until Philip had given him a prod. Her manners were very polite, and she was such a beautiful girl. Her looks were exactly like her mother, with beautiful black hair, and very dark eyes, but there was a subtle difference. Maybe because she was so young, she didn't have the sultry and provocative air about her that Sadie had always used to her advantage. She had a refreshing naivety, which he found very appealing, and she spoke beautifully.

"Good afternoon," she said shyly, smiling gently at them both.

Alan noted she looked them straight in the face, which was always a good sign.

"May I call you Dee?" asked Alan, trying to make her feel at ease.

"Yes, certainly."

Behind Nathan stood Lydia and Jack, and Alan glanced over at them, wondering if he should banish the rest of the family and speak to Dee in private. Nathan looked as if he might chip in if he thought Dee needed some support.

Dee saw her family standing by the door, and it felt comforting to know they cared about her. She had by now overcome her shyness, so she took control of the situation.

"Sir, I have nothing to hide, so my family don't need to be sent out of the room. I am happy for them to hear anything that I have to say."

Alan admired her quiet confidence. She had an air of honesty about her, and her innocence was appealing. She seemed a mixture of maturity and naivety, which was endearing, or did she have him fooled, and was she a very good actress? He decided to continue to observe her reactions whilst he questioned her.

He turned towards Wendy, making sure that she was included. A woman's angle was always useful, especially when dealing with teenage girls.

"This is Wendy. She will be taking notes about our conversation today."

Dee shook hands with Wendy politely, and Nathan and Jack moved further into the room, and stood at the side. Lydia decided to make some tea.

"I am going to put the kettle on. Make yourselves comfortable."

Everyone sat down, and Lydia took note of what they all wanted. Alan decided to wait until she returned with the tea before he questioned Dee.

"What a lovely view of the sea," he commented.

"Yes, and it's such a nice day, I might as well open the doors," said Nathan enthusiastically.

When he opened the patio doors, they all followed him outside to the terrace, where there was a big wooden table, with several chairs. Benches were also ranged behind them, as this was the best area to sit in the sunshine and get a maximum view of the sea.

Lydia appeared with a tray of refreshments, which were duly served out to everyone. Alan took a sip of his tea, and then said casually.

"Dee, can you tell me in your own words about your movements on Friday after you returned from school?"

Dee's eyes held him; she looked him straight in the face, and spoke with complete honesty.

"I got home from school about four thirty, then I left about fifteen minutes later to meet Beth, to go to the cinema."

"Are you sure about the time?"

"Yes, the film started at five, and we only just made it."

Alan turned towards the others. "Can any of you confirm this timing?

Lydia and Jack both nodded, then Jack spoke.

"I always get in minutes after Dee because I ride my bike home, and that would be right. I took a drink up to her room just before she went out."

Alan turned back towards Dee. "Do you know what time you left the cinema?"

Dee looked thoughtful. "I think it was some time after six. It wasn't a long film, but sorry I can't remember exactly."

"What did you do after that?"

"Beth and I got some chips and a drink, then we walked along the downs. I do remember we met Janet, very briefly, and we thought maybe she was going to meet Billy."

"Did you ask her?"

"No, I didn't say much to her, Beth just told her the film was very funny. After she had gone, we carried on walking until we got to the bus stop, and I saw Beth onto her bus home. I wasn't ready to go home then, so I walked towards Reculver, but when I got near to the headland I started to feel dizzy. It's a place I have not visited for a long time. I stayed on the beach as I passed it. I remember the tide was quite high, just starting to go out again, and then I saw Billy on the beach."

Alan remembered what he had been told about her fear of the headland, so he spoke kindly to her. "Did you speak to Billy?"

"Of course, but by then I was feeling so dizzy. I kept trying to fight it, and I remember asking him to help me."

"And did he?"

"Well, he did try. He gave me a puff of the cigarette he was smoking, but after that it becomes blank and I just don't remember any more."

Nathan's face showed his annoyance, and judging by Dee's body language she had expected that. Jack was in awe of her courage in admitting she had been smoking, knowing how Nathan and Lydia had both warned them of the peril in doing it. Dee was full of surprises, and not as meek as she appeared sometimes.

Dee knew how upset Nathan would be, and decided her best means of defence would be attack, so she turned towards him and declared.

"Before you ask me; no, I don't smoke, Daddy, but in that

moment, I would have done anything to stop myself from fainting. I realise it was the wrong thing to do, and it will never happen again, so does Billy, and he has promised me he will try to give up."

This took the wind right out of Nathan's sails. "Well, thanks for telling us that, and being completely honest."

Alan continued to appraise her. "Is there any particular reason why you didn't want to go home, and ended up walking in an area which up until now you had avoided?" he asked, continuing to watch her very carefully.

Dee blushed. She still felt embarrassed by her behaviour towards Lydia that day, and escaping through the conservatory. It had been a very childish and rebellious thing to do. But it didn't stop her from speaking clearly to explain.

"Beth had invited me to go to the cinema with her. I knew other girls from my class would be there, and she was my only friend, so it felt important to me to go. But Lydia wanted me to do my homework. . ." she paused, and addressed her step mother. "And you were right. I should have done it, and I should not have been so rude to you."

"It's OK Dee, you were under a lot of stress. I get it," said Lydia very generously.

"Go on," prompted Alan. This was very interesting.

"So I locked my bedroom door after Jack had left me, so he didn't know, and I left the house, escaping through the conservatory. My parents didn't know, they thought I was revising like I should have been. I knew I couldn't go home until it was dark, as hopefully by then they would be settled up the other end of the house watching TV."

"I see." Her words took Alan totally by surprise. So she wasn't a miss goody two shoes, she was a normal rebellious teenager. She did have it in her, after all.

"I know I behaved badly, and if I hadn't fainted on that beach, you wouldn't be here now. But I never saw Janet there, only Billy, and then after that it all becomes blank."

"Can you remember where you were when you met Billy on the beach? Was it by the cave entrance?"

"No, the tide had turned, I was further down the beach, walking on the wet sand. It's always a bit rocky underfoot by the caves. I don't know how I was found there."

Alan and Wendy, who was busy taking notes, exchanged glances. So it looked like Billy had dragged unconscious Dee up to the cave entrance to stop her being caught up when the tide turned and came in again. So Billy wasn't all bad. Alan reckoned when Billy gave his fingerprints they would match those in the phone box, but he said nothing.

Nathan moved to put his arm round Dee's shoulders. She was forgiven as far as he was concerned. She had come clean about being victimised to them, and now she had told DCI Clarke about escaping from the house, and admitted it was bad behaviour. He could never doubt her honesty.

Alan turned towards Wendy, and she nodded her head and stopped taking notes.

"Well, thank you very much Dee for explaining everything to us. I am sure you are aware just how supportive your family are."

He glanced around, including Jack in his gaze, and noted the boy was smiling at Dee. It struck him that this family might not be joined together by blood ties, but they were certainly joined by loyalty and love.

"I think we have enough information for now. I just need to interview your friend Beth, but I don't seem to have her address on this printout. Beth Harper, is that her name?"

"Yes, that is her name. I have never been to her house, but she lives on the riverside estate at Greenhill. I know I can text her and get it," offered Dee.

Dee sent Beth a text explaining that the police wanted to speak to her, so could she have her exact address. Her reply came back very quickly. Beth was out, but she would be happy to meet up with the police in the picnic area at Reculver.

"She's not at home, and nor is anyone else in the family, but she can meet you at Reculver," explained Dee.

It was highly unusual for a witness to set the meeting point, and Alan pondered on whether to leave the interview until the next day. Maybe he should go back now, but then he remembered that Ruth and Gerald were taking Zoe and Adam to meet some friends, so the house would be empty. So he came to a quick decision.

"OK, tell me exactly where we will be meeting her, and we will go right now."

Chapter Ten

As they travelled to Reculver in the car, Alan discussed the interview with Wendy.

"What did you make of Dee? Did you trust her?"

"She seemed to be a really nice girl. She owned up to her argument with Lydia, and seemed genuinely sorry. I believed her. What about you?"

Alan shook his head. "I am really not sure. She looks like her mother, but seems much quieter and reserved. Yes, she seemed contrite, but was she fooling us all? I was very charmed by her apparent honesty and nice manners, but when I heard she had defied her stepmother, and escaped from the house, it somehow didn't fit in with the picture I had of her. Is she just a great little actress?"

"Well, don't forget she felt under pressure because of the taunting. Desperation made her go out, I think."

"You may well be right, Wendy. My heart tells me she is a well brought up and pleasant young lady, but my policeman's head tells me I must be suspicious."

They had by now arrived at Reculver, and passed by the lane where Philip and Isabel lived. They spotted the ruins of the Reculver Towers, which stood proud against the skyline, and then they found the car park, which was very full.

Alan found a space at the end of the row, and went to get a ticket; he felt an hour would easily be long enough. They saw all the people sitting outside the King Ethelbert pub, talking and laughing, and the playground was full of children playing happily.

Outside the playground stood a young girl, very pretty with her blonde hair in plaits. She surveyed them, and hesitated. Wendy went over to her, saying softly, "Are you Beth?"

"Yes, I am."

Alan noted her ready smile, and her blue eyes sparkled with innocence. He had been surprised that she wanted to meet them in public like this, but Beth soon took charge of the situation.

"Hi, it's a bit noisy here, and not at all private, shall we walk down the slipway to the beach?"

"Lead on, you know the way," said Alan.

Wendy was glad, although she was dressed casually, that she had her sturdy lace-up shoes on, as they negotiated the rough path down to the beach. Alan was very aware that somewhere on this beach Janet's body had been found, and Dee had fainted. Yet with the tide now going out, and sand and rock pools all around them, and the rugged cliffs above, it looked a friendly and welcoming seaside resort.

Beth found a cave area by the cliffs which was empty. This was certainly unusual, but curiosity made Alan go along with it.

"We can sit here," said Beth, pointing to some rocks. "How was Dee when you saw her?" Her face showed anxiety.

"She was fine," said Wendy reassuringly.

"Was it near here that Janet's body was found?" asked Alan, as they had yet to visit the crime scene. He had decided interviewing was more important, especially as the sea had washed any evidence away.

"Poor Janet," sighed Beth. Her blue eyes looked so sad. "No, it was further up towards Bishopstone Glen, about a mile from here, and Dee as well, of course."

"Yes, did you know Janet well?"

"Not really, I am a close friend to Dee."

Alan studied her face, which registered concern. She looked sad. She was a typical English rose, with her blonde hair and blue eyes.

"Did you know that Dee had an argument with her stepmother before she met you on Friday afternoon?"

Beth's eyes registered surprise. "She never said. We just went to see the film. It was a funny one, and we saw some other girls from our school."

"What did you do after that?"

"We got chips, and then sat down and ate them. But I should have realised when she commented that this was as close to home as she dared go. I realised time was getting on, so I said I should be going home, and Dee said she was going for a walk. But she saw me onto the bus first, and said she didn't mind me going."

"Didn't you think it was strange that she wasn't going home?"

"Not at the time, although I can see it now. It was such a lovely evening."

"Did you meet anyone else during your walk?"

"Yes, we saw Janet, and she was heading towards the beach. I thought she might have been meeting Billy, as he had come over again; he's always flying back and forth."

"It seems you and Dee were among the last people to see Janet alive. How did she seem?"

Beth wrinkled her brow in an effort to remember. "She seemed OK, quite happy actually, which is why I thought she might be meeting Billy. She was very keen on him."

"Well thanks for all this," said Alan. "I still didn't get your address, it's missing from the form."

Beth hesitated, and to Alan's practised eyes she looked awkward, but only for a brief second.

"I live at twenty-four Riverside Walk. It's the new estate over at Greenhill."

Wendy wrote it down, and Beth repeated her mobile number.

"Well, many thanks Beth, we now know how to contact you if we need to, but that is all we need for now."

"Yes, on the mobile is best, none of us are at home much. My parents work long hours, and we don't have a landline."

Alan nodded his thanks, and they both watched her bound up the slope, skilfully avoiding all the uneven parts. It was obvious she was well used to negotiating the rocky beach.

A glance at his watch showed Alan it was now one o'clock, and he realised if he headed back to Whitstable, he could catch up with his family. They had interviewed three witnesses since they had arrived yesterday, and first thing tomorrow they would report to Canterbury Police Station to meet the rest of the team, all eager to help them with this investigation. But there was just one more thing to do.

"Have you got details of the exact location of the crime scene?" he asked Wendy. "Maybe we should visit it on the way home."

"Yes sir. It may still be cordoned off, but the sea has washed away any footprints."

"I know. We will just take a look, and then it's the afternoon off for us both."

This was music to Wendy's ears. It had been full on since they arrived, and she was looking forward to strolling along the downs at Tankerton. There was a little hut, which was a cafe, at the end, with tables both outside and in, and she wanted to sit outside with a cup of coffee, and enjoy her lunch overlooking the sea.

This area was such a change after the busyness of the London suburbs, with cars everywhere, buses trundling along and lorries giving out unpleasant fumes. Here she could enjoy nice clean fresh air. Even though her reason for being here was not a holiday, one very precious restful afternoon was beckoning, followed by dinner at her hotel and then enjoying the comfort of her suite, and she couldn't wait.

When Alan arrived back at his in-laws house, it was empty. He rang Zoe, who explained that they were all sitting out in the garden with Les and Lena, who were friends of her parents, eating Pizza.

"Oh, that sounds great. I am starving, you know."

"Well, come round and join us, there is plenty for everyone."

Alan took down the address and postcode. His grumbling stomach couldn't wait for him to drive round there, and he arrived within a few minutes. He was introduced to Les and Lena, a couple in their fifties, who were very active in the local community. They were part of the neighbourhood watch team, and also Lena ran a fitness club, which was where Ruth had met her.

"I admire you working on a Sunday. Why not sit down and have a beer now," said Les hospitably.

"I think maybe a shandy. I have got the car," said Alan.

"I can drive it back, don't worry," said Zoe, pressing his hand. She felt Alan deserved to relax with a couple of beers. In this beautiful sunshine, with the birds chirping, it was easy to forget what a stressful job he had, but she knew.

Alan glanced over at Adam sleeping peacefully in his pushchair, obviously the sea air was doing him good. Les handed him a beer, and he sipped it, enjoying the feel of the cool liquid running down inside him. He had not realised how thirsty he was. Zoe put a big slice of pepperoni pizza on his plate, adding a little salad garnish, which made him smile.

"So you've all had a great morning then?" he said, smiling at them all.

"Yes, and Adam fell asleep on his way round here," explained Zoe.

"I have yet to hold him," said Lena, wistfully.

"Lena and Les have grandchildren in Scotland, so they don't see them that often," said Ruth.

"We do most of the visiting, but it always seems to be cold and rainy there. We keep saying they should come here for a holiday."

"They are coming in the school holidays," Les reminded her.

"Yes, in July, it can't come soon enough. The youngest will be walking by then I expect!"

By the time Alan had finished eating, Adam had woken up. Ruth picked him up out of his pushchair, and handed him to Lena, whose face lit up with pleasure.

"Nothing like holding a baby, is there?" she said, cradling him so gently.

Alan could see he was being spoiled. They usually waited until he cried before they picked him up, but he felt quite cool about it. Wasn't that what grandparents did? It wasn't long before Ruth took over; it seemed she couldn't get enough of her grandson.

Zoe sat watching them until her son puckered up his face, and let out a wail.

"He's due for a feed now," she said, jumping out of her seat.

"You can sit in the lounge. It's nice and quiet in there," said Lena.

Alan watched Zoe disappear inside before he spoke. Coming

here had been a great idea, she looked much more relaxed already, and Ruth and Gerald were very happy to have them. He had always got on well with her parents, and it was nice they understood that having their own unit upstairs was great, because sometimes he just wanted Zoe and Adam to himself. He could not remember the last time they had been out; it was a good few months, so this might be an opportunity.

"I know Zoe is breastfeeding, and won't want to leave Adam for too long but. . ."

"Yes, of course we will babysit," said Ruth, reading his thoughts.

"I could take her out for a meal tonight."

"Lots of great pubs in Whitstable, then there's the Sportsman, but you might not get in at short notice."

"I'll ask her when she comes back."

They sat idly chatting until Zoe returned with Adam, who looked very sleepy and contented. She handed him to Alan, guessing he would have missed his son, and would not get a look in with two very maternal women there as well.

"Make sure he hasn't any wind. You are so good at burping him."

Alan's heart swelled with pride. Until six weeks ago, babies had been a complete mystery to him, but together with Zoe, he felt he was learning about his son every day. He held him against his chest and patted his back, slowly walking up and down, until he was rewarded with a loud burp.

"Oh, well done!" exclaimed the women in unison, and Alan smiled to himself, thinking he would not have got the same reaction if he had done that. He turned towards Zoe, and tried to sound casual, as though it wasn't a very big deal.

"Do you fancy going out for dinner tonight? Just a couple of hours between Adam's feeds."

Zoe walked over and took her sleeping son, placing him in his pushchair whilst considering Alan's words. After only six weeks, and the bond that had been formed even more by breastfeeding him, Zoe still felt as though she couldn't be parted from Adam. Her tiny helpless son needed her, and in the evening was his most restless time. Was it even fair to inflict it on her parents?

But then she looked at the bigger picture. Alan was also her world, and he had willingly taken a back seat ever since Adam had been born. Not only that, when they eventually returned home, there would not be an opportunity to go out, because she was certainly not going to leave her young son with a stranger.

"Mum, you know how fussy he is in the evening?" she reminded Ruth.

"Your mother just wants an excuse to cuddle him," said Gerald, his eyes twinkling.

"You are just as bad!" remarked Ruth. "Thanks to modern technology we can send you a text and a photo, so you can see how he's getting on."

That seemed to make up Zoe's mind, so she gave Alan a spontaneous hug.

"Oh, yes please, it will be lovely!"

"I will try and book somewhere. What do you fancy?"

"Anywhere with you, even if it's fish and chips on the beach."

They both laughed, like teenagers going on a date, and Ruth and Gerald looked on. It was about time Zoe went out, and they were pleased to see her smiling. Being a new mum wasn't easy, but their girl was doing very well.

Chapter Eleven

On Monday the weather changed. It was a grey day with fine rain, but still very muggy. Mist could be seen on the horizon, and the fine rain covered the grass areas, and dampened the paths and streets. After a few days of the promise of summer to come, this was not a welcome sight.

Dee returned to school and, in spite of the weather, she did not return with the same dread in her heart that she had experienced before. She knew instinctively that her life at school would be much easier now. When she arrived at school, Beth was waiting for her outside the gates, and now the other girls spoke to her when she passed them. Some even came up and asked her how she was. The words from the head had created the desired effect.

Right from the first day, she found she could concentrate much better in class. And her desire to do her homework and do well had returned. She hadn't done very well in her mock exams, and she had less than two weeks left to swot and catch up, but she vowed to herself that she was going to do her very best, and not waste a minute of the time she had left.

When Jack came home and found her revising in her room, he was pleased for her. She was obviously feeling on top of things.

"Sis, if I knew you were being got at, I could have helped, you know. Now I understand why you deleted your Facebook page."

"I know, I allowed it to get on top of me, and I tried to cope on my own. The only person who did know was Beth, and she did support me, but it still didn't stop."

"Well, now they need to find the person who killed Janet. But if she bullied others the way she bullied you, then it could honestly be anyone in your class."

"Yes, someone who lost their temper with her? They might not have meant to kill her," suggested Dee.

"Which brings me back to Billy. I've seen him having a paddy, and it's not a pretty sight."

Dee didn't want to think it was Billy. After all, they were related, so her natural instinct was to defend him.

"I know you don't like Billy 'cos he is arrogant, and I am not close to him, but I don't see him as a murderer, more a spoiled young man. If you are talking about that time he had a paddy when he had to go home, and yet he wanted to stay for Christmas, he didn't actually hit anyone."

"No, but he pumelled the wall hard, and broke a couple of cups that he threw. Sometimes I think you are too nice, Dee, you think everyone is kind like you."

Dee changed the subject. It didn't feel comfortable or right openly discussing Billy.

"I may reinstate my facebook page again, but I will give it a few more days just to be sure."

"That is good news," said Jack warmly, "and now I will leave you to get on with your revising."

Alan and Wendy reported to Canterbury Police Station on Monday for a debriefing. A team of officers were there, and they were introduced to them. Alan pinned up photographs of the witnesses he had interviewed so far onto the board, and then proceeded to address everyone.

"Dee Edwards, daughter of the late Sadie Morton Brown, a quiet and well mannered girl when we interviewed her. Didn't appear to be much of a rebel until we found out she had escaped from the house, and gone to the cinema after her stepmother had forbidden it. She was being bullied by Janet, who had found out about her mother's past and then proceeded to taunt her with it. Dee was found very close to Janet's body, but claims to know nothing about

e

how she got there. Interestingly, she reckons she passed out further down the beach, and some unknown as yet, person, dragged her body up the beach, and put it close to Janet, either to frame her, or to save her from the incoming tide. Obviously she has to be a suspect, as killing Janet would free her from being bullied. From what I saw, she doesn't seem to have that sort of aggression in her, but maybe she is just a very good actress."

Alan then moved the tip of his pen to point towards the photograph of Billy.

"Billy Hopkins, half brother to Dee from Sadie's first marriage to Ricky Scott. She had him adopted after she left Ricky. He was adopted by Jill and Simon Hopkins, who were childless, and in later years, Ricky found his son, and made contact. When Philip and Isabel Morton Brown found they had a grandson, after Sadie's untimely death, he became part of the family, jetting back and forth across the Atlantic Ocean for visits. He was Janet's boyfriend, and was not impressed when she told him she was pregnant. We found him to be arrogant, and not particularly helpful when we made our inquiries."

Constable Gary Hill entered the room with a sheaf of papers in his hand.

"Sir, we have several pieces of information about Billy Hopkins. Firstly, his fingerprints match those found in the call box at Manor Road, and he has a police record in the States for minor crimes such as car theft, but he was also accused of assault outside a bar one night by a man who was apparently paying too much attention to his girlfriend at the time, Barbara Carter. It was alleged he hit him and broke his nose, but later the charge was withdrawn."

Alan looked very thoughtful. "Well, I guessed that Billy moved his sister up the beach, so that part doesn't surprise me, but I do wonder why the charge was withdrawn."

"The man withdrew it; his name is Terry Harris, and Barbara Carter is no longer with Billy, she is married to Harris."

"Thanks for that, Hill. I wonder if we could speak to him by video link. It's a long way to travel to speak to a witness."

"I will try and arrange it for you, sir."

Alan addressed the team, as Gary left the room. His pen now

travelled to the photograph of Beth Harper, and he turned towards them.

"Beth Harper is the closest friend to Dee Edwards. She is the same age, and in the same class at school. She appears to care a lot about Dee, and gives the impression of being a very friendly and smiley sort of person. She is also very good at controlling a situation, as Wendy and I found out when she suggested where we should meet. The only reservation I had about her is she didn't seem keen on us coming to her house. She said she was out and so were both her parents, yet it was Sunday. But she did willingly give us her mobile number after saying they didn't have a landline. Dee is her alibi, as she saw her onto the bus home to Greenhill, where she says she lives.

"She's a teenager, so maybe she didn't want her parents to know she was being interviewed," suggested Wendy.

"Yes, that occurred to me as well, and as for the rest of the class, all twenty-seven of them, I have not personally interviewed them, but I understand local police did, and every single one of them has an alibi. Although some were with each other, so we don't know for sure they are all telling the truth."

Gary returned to the room explaining that he had contacted the FBI, who were going to get in touch with Terry and Barbara and arrange for them to be interviewed by video link.

"Well done, Hill, that was quick. It's only about seven in the morning over there, isn't it?" Alan enquired.

"Yes, but they have someone on standby twenty-four hours a day," said Gary, pleased that his new temporary boss thought he was efficient. "They are going to call us when it's all set up, and they are aiming for two o'clock this afternoon our time."

"That's just a couple of hours, so I suggest we all have our lunch now, and meet back here in an hour," said Alan.

Everyone dispersed, and Wendy went out to buy them some coffee. Alan had brought sandwiches, which Zoe had prepared earlier. After a very enjoyable evening out last night, she had got up early, whilst Adam was sleeping, to see him off to work. He had tried to stop her, saying she needed all the rest she could get, but Zoe was determined.

Today it was ham and tomato, and a pork pie, also a banana and a Twix bar. Not too much salad today, and Alan loved the way she was mothering him. Zoe and Adam made his life complete, and he knew he was a very lucky man.

Dave Kent thought it was time he contacted Ricky, after his head office had informed him why they wanted to contact Terry and Barbara Harris. He was very aware of the difficult times his best friend had suffered, as he had visited England with him on a couple of occasions.

The first time had been to interview Alice, the nanny of the Morton Brown family. The second occasion was the day when Sadie was so tragically killed. He had accompanied Ricky because Ricky had taken the decision to visit Sadie, and tell her that he had made contact with their son Billy, and there were no hard feelings, and she would be welcome to meet him if she wanted to. Knowing Ricky, he would have taken him over there to make it as easy as possible for her.

Sadly Ricky had never been able to say those words, as Sadie had met her death when she was hit by a van. Dave felt that Ricky didn't deserve all the things that had happened to him. First his beautiful wife Amy, and mother of his three girls, had been killed in a car crash, and Ricky had to try and hold down his job in the FBI whilst bringing up three very lively daughters. Then he thought he had found happiness again with Sadie, but the marriage hadn't lasted, and it had left him and the girls heartbroken. Ricky was such a nice guy and he had borne Sadie no ill will, then he had witnessed her tragic death.

As if that wasn't enough, his son Billy was damaged by the situation. Ricky had done his best to keep Billy on the right path. He definitely needed to know the British police were wanting to trace Terry and Barbara and interview them.

Dave knew all about Billy's assault, Ricky had confided in him, and he realised that cops being cops, they would want to link it with the murder of that girl on the beach. The details of that had been broadcast all over the world. It was typical how trouble seemed to follow Billy around, and he just happened to be staying in that area when it happened.

Ricky had felt uneasy ever since he had read about the young girl found on the beach near Herne Bay. He knew that Philip and Isabel had paid for Billy to go over and visit them as he had recently dropped out of college. It was incredible that it had happened whilst Billy was there; in fact, on the same day that he had arrived.

Not for a moment did he think his son was involved; it was just bad timing. He was actually thinking of contacting Philip to suggest maybe it would be best if Billy came home, and he could go back later when things had calmed down. He was having a few days leave, so he could pick him up from the airport and take him home. His cell phone rang and interrupted his thoughts.

"Hi buddy, what's new?" he asked.

"Ricky, we just had a call from the British police. They want to trace Terry and Barbara Carter to interview them on Skype. It's connected to the murder of the girl on the beach at Herne Bay."

Ricky felt an ice cold hand clutching at his heart. No, it couldn't be Billy, surely?"

"I have to get over there, Dave, but how does this connect with Billy? I don't get it."

Dave swallowed, wishing he didn't have to tell him, poor guy!

"Billy was dating the girl who died, so they did a police check on him and found out about his petty crime. There was also a record of the assault charge. Even though it was dropped, the file was never closed."

"Thanks for filling me in, buddy. I am right over on the first flight I can get. I won't be in for a few days."

"Of course, good luck man. Let me know how it goes," said Dave.

Ricky cleared down. There was no time to waste, Billy needed him right now. He went online to arrange a flight, luckily he could get one this evening, which meant he would be in England early tomorrow morning. He prayed that the police would not conduct an interview without him, because Billy might need a solicitor. Ricky was going to make sure his son had all the support he could give him.

Alan and Gary had the computer all set up for the Skype call in the afternoon, and Wendy stood nearby to make notes about the conversation. Dave Kent came on first to explain that Terry and Barbara were there with them, and ready to be interviewed.

"Thank you so much," said Alan, and into view came a man about thirty with reddish brown hair. His companion was younger, maybe early twenties, she had brown straight hair with a full fringe and brown eyes. They both looked very worried.

Alan greeted them in a friendly manner in an effort to put them at ease, and then explained that he had heard about the assault on Terry some two years ago, and wondered if they could tell him more about it. They both looked nervously at each other, and then Terry spoke.

"Yes sir, two years ago my wife Barbara was dating Billy, but it was not going well. She wanted to be free of him, and told me he had a quick temper. We became close, then Billy found out. He lost his temper and hit me outside a bar when I was going home."

"Did you hit him back?"

"Yes sir, in my defence, but he busted my nose."

"So you instigated charges against him, but then you dropped them. Why was that?"

Terry coloured visibly, then hesitated. "Well, nobody else saw him break my nose, and he also had injuries, a black eye. Barbara and I just wanted to get wed, and have a normal life. Our attorney said it might be hard to prove, and maybe Billy was provoked. Maybe he was. After all, I stole his girl, didn't I?"

"So nobody paid you to drop the charges then?" asked Alan, remembering just how wealthy Philip was.

"No sir, they did not. We put it behind us, and it was never mentioned again until today."

"OK, many thanks for your time," said Alan, and Dave Kent came back into camera view.

"Thanks for setting this up, Dave," said Alan.

Dave nodded his head. "OK sir, but I don't imagine it's much help in your murder case though."

Alan was thoughtful. "Maybe not, but it proves that Billy Hopkins has an uncontrollable temper."

Dave couldn't wait to end this conversation. It was clear his best friend's son was in the frame, and Ricky was on his way over to England to support him. This wasn't looking good at all. He really hoped Ricky could find a good lawyer to represent Billy, otherwise this young kid was going to be charged with murder. He ended the conversation politely.

"Good afternoon, sir, I wish you every success with your investigation."

"Good afternoon, Kent, and thanks for your help today."

The camera faded off and Alan closed the computer. Wendy put her pen down. The picture they were getting of Billy was not a pleasant one. Arrogant, volatile, and a known lawbreaker in the past.

"What do you reckon about Billy, sir? Maybe he is not all bad, because he did save Dee from being swept out by the tide."

"I am not sure. He could have moved her up the beach to get her framed for Janet's murder; she was very close. It sounds like you couldn't put anything past him. I think we had better get him in for further questioning."

Chapter Twelve

Dee's first day back at school had gone well. It felt like the time before Janet had been there, some two years ago. Her confidence was already growing, especially when Jenny, who had been her friend up until Janet came, became friendly again. She had walked to the bus stop with her to get the bus home. Jenny had invited her to drop round her house when she was free, as it was only in the next road, and minutes away from Dee's.

"We can take my dog Rex out."

"I would love that, maybe along the beach to Reculver," suggested Dee. She had thought about her dizzy spell, and was determined to beat it by confronting it. She had promised daddy she wouldn't walk that way alone until the murder was solved, but she would be with a companion.

Maria was visiting her this evening at the house, and she wanted to be able to tell her that she was facing up to her fears. She now believed that her bad reaction had been because she had stayed away from that area for ten years.

She had tried to put it all into perspective by reminding herself that Alice had been ill, and could have fallen over any one of the cliffs around. It was just unfortunate it had been at the top of her favourite childhood place, the Fairy Bridge at Bishopstone Glen.

For once Beth had not walked to the bus stop with her after school. She had left in the morning after complaining of not feeling well. Dee was concerned about her, so she sent her a text to find out how she was. Beth had replied that she had a bad sore throat and might be coming down with a cold, so she would not be at school until she felt better. So Dee replied telling her about going home on the bus with Jenny, and their plans to go for a walk. She said how happy she was that people were treating her normally again.

She was surprised to receive another text from Beth, this time suggesting that it might be better if she didn't visit Bishopstone Glen again, or even walk that way, because of what happened before. She did not reply to this one, other than to say she hoped Beth would feel better soon.

In her own mind Dee felt she could cope. Just because she had a quiet nature, it didn't mean that she wasn't prepared to face challenges in her life, and this was a big one for her. Now that the pressure from Janet had been removed, it made her want to overcome her fears.

When she arrived home from school, she told Lydia about her day. She felt happy, and then she mentioned Jenny to Lydia.

"Oh, I remember Jenny. So glad she is friendly with you again. And that sounds like a good idea, as long as you stay together, if you feel ready for it," Lydia replied. Seeing Dee so animated, with colour in her cheeks, felt like they were getting the real Dee back, and that was great. Nathan would be so happy when he got home.

Dee remembered she was having a visitor. "What time is Maria coming?" she enquired.

"In about half an hour. You have got time for a snack," replied Lydia.

"Thanks Lydia, you are a star! I am going to do a bit of French revising until she gets here."

"Good girl! Jack will be home soon. Do you fancy some toast or something to tide you over?"

"Can I have a toasted teacake, and a cold drink?"

Lydia went into the kitchen to make the snack whilst Dee headed off into the conservatory, clutching her knapsack full of books. As far as Lydia was concerned, she could have anything she wanted, and she wasn't even going to complain about waiting on her, or remind her she was perfectly capable of getting her own snack. Dee was happy, and she was eating; that was absolutely a step in the right direction.

She knew Nathan was on his way home now, and he would be anxious about how her first day at school had been, but he had no need to be. It was very sad that it had taken the tragic death of Janet for everything to get back to normal, and she really did feel for what Janet's parents must be going through, but it was such a relief to see Dee coping with life again.

Alan and Wendy were in the car, on their way to see Billy again. As they travelled up through the village of Beltinge, on the way to Reculver, Alan was still thinking about their interview with Beth yesterday. She had struck him as being very self-possessed, and it could be that she didn't want her parents to know she was being interviewed again. But there was still a niggling doubt. Why had she not been keen to reveal her home address? He felt they should check it out.

Of course, if there was no one in, it would tell them nothing. Beth said her parents worked long hours, and she would be at school, but it was on the way, and there would probably be neighbours around, so they could ask them who lived there.

"Wendy, I have decided, I want to check out twenty-four Riverside Walk. Do we have a postcode?"

"I was thinking the same thing, sir. No postcode, but I can Google it on my phone."

Wendy quickly found the postcode, and it wasn't long before they were driving down the road. It was a pretty housing estate, with houses built to look old fashioned in keeping with the area. The estate was set near to the river Stour, and there was parkland and trees, with a children's playground at the end of the road.

Today being grey and misty meant there were no mothers with young children in the play park. It stood empty; the slide had raindrops falling on it, and the swings were damp, which gave it an air of neglect.

"There is number twenty-four," said Wendy, pointing at the house at the end of the section of buildings. It had conifers at the side so no one could look into the front garden as they were passing, and there was no car in the drive. Although the houses were

106

detached, there were only a few inches between the garages set at the side of the houses. Alan guessed there would be a door from the garage into the house. The conifer hedge stretched across the small front garden, separating it from the communal walkway which led to the other houses. Because of the way the conifers had been set out, this house was a bit more private than the others.

"I don't think there will be much chance of rousing anyone. No car in the drive," pointed out Alan, whilst walking towards the door.

"Oh well, we are here, so we might as well try," said Wendy hopefully.

Alan rang the doorbell, and they both stood there as the rain continued to drizzle. Not a sound could be heard from inside. As Alan expected, it seemed that no one was at home.

"Come on, we are wasting our time," he said briskly.

"Wait, I heard something," said Wendy.

Alan was not convinced by her words, and started to walk up the path, but as he turned to look back, the door opened just a fraction, and Beth's face peeped out. Alan was so shocked, without even thinking, he said, "What are you doing? You should be in school."

Beth's voice sounded husky. "I have a sore throat and a nasty cold. I really don't feel well. Why are you here?"

Alan was momentarily caught off guard, but luckily Wendy spoke to save the situation.

"We forgot to ask you yesterday, how long have you known Dee? Did you go to primary school together?"

"We used to live in Brighton, and we moved here two years ago, and that is how long I have known Dee."

"Thanks very much. We are done now, and we hope you feel better soon."

Wendy smiled at Beth as she spoke, glad they had found her in; that cleared up another puzzle. She followed Alan down the path and back to the car.

Beth was so glad to see them go. By peeping from behind the door, they hadn't been able to see that she was in full school uniform, and she thought she had done a good job of making her voice sound husky.

She knew she was lucky that Ian still cared about her, and paid her school fees, because without his support she would not have been able to go to St Martha's. For the past year she had kept up the pretence that she and her mother still lived at that address, but her mother had managed to ruin that. Ian had been good for her mother, but Lizzie just had to mess the relationship up in her inimitable way. It was the story of their life so far.

There was no way Beth would let anyone discover her secret. It was a matter of pride. Luckily she knew that Ian would be at work at this time of day, and even if he had been there having an unexpected day off, she still had her door key. He had said she was welcome any time, and would have been pleased that she had visited him.

Ricky had managed to get a flight from New York to Heathrow, which arrived first thing on Tuesday morning. He hadn't managed to snatch much sleep,and he couldn't wait to get in a shower and clean up. After picking up his luggage, and then negotiating passport control and customs, he was met by a driver to be taken straight to Herne Bay. He was booked into the Premier Inn at Beltinge, which was only a few minutes drive from Philip and Isabel's home.

The sun was out this morning and the streets were drying after the rain of Monday, but he scarcely noticed the weather. His only concern was Billy. That young man might already be in custody, and he would need to find him a good solicitor.

Billy was certainly making hard work of growing up, but Ricky did not believe that he was a murderer. Working for the FBI as he did, he knew the cops would find anything they could against someone who was a suspect, and them finding out that Billy was volatile had not helped his case at all.

He checked into his room, and left his suitcase there. Even now, he had no intention of resting; anxiety had overcome weariness, and he was desperate to see Billy. He asked the taxi to wait whilst he spoke to Philip on his cell phone, there was no sense in turning up if there was no one there.

Ricky had not seen Philip for ten years, not since Sadie's funeral, although they had kept in touch because of Billy. It had all seemed so unreal at the time, and he had forgiven her everything because he was not a vindictive man. Her untimely death had been such a tragedy, and he had really felt for Nathan, who clearly had loved her very deeply.

He had Philip's number, so he called it, and was relieved when Philip spoke.

"Hi Philip, it's Ricky here, I thought I would take a vacation and see Billy. Is he there?"

"I am afraid not, Ricky, he is at the police station helping them with their inquiries. I offered to go with him, but the police said it was only a formality."

Ricky drew a breath, maybe he was worrying over nothing, just a formality sounded OK.

"I know about the girl on the beach, and I heard he was dating her. He never spoke about her at home."

"I think it was a holiday romance. Billy didn't speak as though it was serious. Why don't you come round, Ricky, we can put our heads together and see how we can help him."

"OK, I have a car here ready. I am staying at the Premier Inn."

"You don't need to stay there, we have room for you."

"You are very kind, but it's all booked."

After he came off the phone, Philip explained to Isabel that Ricky was in England, and now on his way over. They had not known, until Sadie died, that he had once been their son-in-law. And he was also their grandson's father, so he still felt like one of the family. They had welcomed Billy into their family, and now that it looked like he was in trouble, all they wanted to do was help him.

"We will have to tell Ricky that Janet was pregnant," Isabel reminded him.

It had been an unwelcome shock when the police had asked Billy to accompany them to the station for more questioning. Isabel couldn't help remembering his white face and pleading dark eyes when they took him away. Philip had offered to go too, but they had said there was no need, it was purely routine.

But they felt desperate to help him, and Isabel had suggested employing the services of a solicitor, with a very good reputation for winning cases, to help him. But Philip was more cautious, he said they should wait, because Billy might not even be charged. Who could know for sure how many other people were being interviewed, and had motive? Billy was more than likely not the only one.

Alan sat watching Billy across the table. All his arrogance was gone, his attitude was desperate, and fear registered in his eyes. To Alan he looked incredibly guilty.

"Well Billy, your fingerprints match up to those found in the call box at Manor Road, so we know it was you who dragged Dee up the beach after she collapsed."

"Yes, sir."

"I am glad you have had the sense to own up."

"She fainted in front of me, and I thought I would get the blame, so I dragged her to where I thought she would be safe, then went to call an ambulance."

"But why would you get the blame?"

Billy wondered how the hell he would get out of this one. Cops found out everything, nothing in your life stayed private. Then they would ask where he got his stash from. Oh my, he was absolutely in the shit now, but lying would make it worse.

"I was smoking pot and I gave her a puff to help calm her, but she fainted. Please, sir, if my family find out about that I am finished!"

Alan could see he was telling the truth this time, even though it was reluctantly, but where had he got it from? It had to be stopped. He could imagine Nathan would have a heart attack if he knew his little daughter had been smoking pot!

"Well Billy, if you tell me the truth about everything, including where you got this drug, maybe I will spare you the humiliation of telling your family. I don't think Nathan would be impressed to know what you gave to Dee."

"I know, sir, I got it from a man down near the caravans at Reculver. I just wanted to try it. I don't know his name, he was passing through, and I had some money on me because I had just arrived in England. I was going to smoke it with Janet, if she wanted to, I thought it might be fun."

Alan studied him. That look of desperation made him believe Billy. Dealers were notoriously difficult to trace, and convict, so he wasn't going to deviate from this murder inquiry. But at least Billy had made a clumsy attempt to save Dee; or was he cunning, and had moved her to try and frame her? He had to keep an open mind about this.

"So, since you saw Dee faint from the effects, you no longer think it's fun I hope!" His voice was stern; he had to keep this little toerag in line.

"No sir, I promise I won't ever try it again!"

Alan had no idea if Billy could keep a promise, but this did explain a bit more about his actions. He decided that if he had been trying to frame her, then surely he would not have owned up to smoking the pot. He would have kept the heat away from himself. He continued with his questioning.

"Did you feel angry when Janet told you she was pregnant?"

"You asked me that before. I didn't know for sure that it was mine."

"Did you say that to Janet?"

"I did, and she took off. She was very angry."

Alan glared at him. Was he really so stupid that he didn't realise how much he had hurt her? Did he have no sense of responsibility whatsoever?

"Billy, she was a sixteen year old girl who had feelings for you! Are you surprised she was angry?"

"No sir, I spoke my mind because it was such a shock. Maybe if she had stayed around we could have talked about it."

Alan ignored that, he was just saying what Alan wanted to hear. It was bullshit!

"We know you have a temper. You attacked Terry Harris and were charged with assault. Did you lose your temper with Janet? After all, with her being pregnant, it would have messed up your chances of going to college in England, wouldn't it?"

Billy went visibly pale, and caught his breath. Those nosy cops now knew everything, and it felt to him that they were determined to pin this on him. He felt really scared now.

111

"Terry withdrew the charge, he hit me too. I don't hit women, and I never touched Janet."

Wendy glanced over at Alan. She knew he was finding Billy hard work. And it would annoy him, even if he thought Billy had done it, that they just didn't have enough to charge him. He had admitted seeing Janet and Dee, and offering her a puff of his cigarette, and he did have a temper, but it wasn't enough.

"How long after Janet stormed off did you see Dee."

"Ten minutes maybe."

They were interrupted by a knock on the door, and in came Gary.

"We have a recording, sir, of a phone call for you to listen to."

Billy groaned inwardly. He had already admitted that he made the call, and dragged Dee up the beach. They really wanted their pound of flesh! He slumped forward, with his head on the desk, and for some inexplicable reason Wendy found herself feeling sorry for him.

"Would you like a cup of tea?" she offered.

Billy shook his head, the damn English seemed to think tea solved everything. He had been honest with them and it still hadn't helped him. He was now convinced he would be thrown in jail.

Alan listened to the recording. The voice was muffled, but there was a slight trace of an American accent. Billy had already admitted doing this, but there was definitely desperation in his voice. Was it because his temper had made him go too far, or was it concern because Dee's family would be furious if they found out he had made her faint?

"Yes, it's definitely Billy, and he has admitted it too. Doesn't he sound desperate? Thanks very much for this Gary."

"It was the emergency operator. She had the foresight to record it."

Alan returned to the room, noting Billy's hunched attitude. This boy seemed at breaking point, he had to act now.

"Right Billy, get it off your chest. After you hit Janet, you tried to save her by reporting she was on the beach. You ran away from the scene. Then you met Dee, who fainted, so in an effort to divert the blame from yourself, you dragged her body up to where Janet lay, and then went to the call box, being careful to report only one girl as being on the beach."

112

Billy raised his head and stared at him. They did think he had killed her, and they were twisting the truth of what happened just to fit him up!

"No, sir, it wasn't like that. It was Dee, my sister. When she fainted, as I explained before, I felt really bad about it. I dragged her up the beach, I have told you that, and left her at the entrance to a small cave so she couldn't drown; it seemed safer. I ran to the red call box in Manor Road and dialled for help."

"Very noble of you!" Alan could not help his sarcastic tone. "All you had to do was use your mobile, then help would have been quicker. Did you honestly think we wouldn't find out that you made the call?"

"Yes sir, I panicked, I should have used my cell phone."

Alan glanced at Wendy, who was busy writing. This boy could be telling the truth; he just couldn't be sure.

"Billy Hopkins, this interview is terminated at two thirty. You can go now, but don't leave the country. You need to stay here so we can contact you at any time."

"Yes sir, thank you, sir."

Billy now found himself trembling with relief. He could go, but he was close to tears. Wendy opened the door for him, and he stumbled through; there was nothing jaunty about him now. She took him to the main desk, where she explained that he was now free to go .

Alan picked up his papers and followed them. Standing at the book-in desk was Philip, accompanied by another man. Philip introduced him.

"This is Ricky Scott, Billy's father."

Alan shook his hand. Ricky looked very anxious, and he guessed he must be really worried.

"Good afternoon, Mr Scott, we have finished interviewing Billy for today, but he must remain in England until we have finished our enquiries."

"Absolutely. I have flown in to take care of Billy," explained Ricky, relieved to see that Billy had been released. "We will both be staying right here."

Chapter Thirteen

Dee went off to school on Tuesday with a newly found confidence. This was partly due to her first day back at school being peaceful and her friendship with Jenny being on again. When she had met with Maria, the previous evening, she had told her she felt she could take control of her life now, and conquer her fear of the Headland.

Maria had been very impressed. She could see in this determined teenager, a strong will to fight her demons and, in her opinion, the poor girl had endured more than her fair share of them. She had been aware of it all, having been Dee's psychologist and counsellor since she was six years old.

She still remembered the little girl who had lost her mother shortly after being reunited with her. Even though it was ten years ago, it had been heartbreaking to see her struggling. She was now becoming a beautiful and confident young woman, thanks to the love and stability given to her by Nathan and Lydia, as well as her loving grandparents.

Yesterday Dee and Maria had decided together that there was no need for further counselling right now. But Dee knew that Maria was there if she ever struggled again, and that was a comforting thought. Confiding in her had always been easy; easier sometimes than Nathan, if she felt it might upset him.

When she got on the bus, Jenny was already on it, having boarded the stop before, so they sat together chatting on the way to school. Jenny was quite a bouncy girl, she reminded her a little of how her mum had been, but there the similarity ended. Jenny had auburn hair, and it had golden lights in it bleached by the sun, her eyes were hazel, and she had a very infectious laugh. She spoke a lot about her dog Rex, she walked him a lot, and she joked about the fact that she had a solid frame and would never be a size eight, even though they spent hours walking on the local beaches and park areas.

"You look fine to me," said Dee warmly.

"We can't all be skinny, and I love my food."

They had got off the bus now, and strolled into the school grounds. Dee's mind wandered, and she was thinking that maybe this evening, when she got home, she would reinstate her Facebook page. Suddenly her life had returned to normal, and it felt so good.

As if reading her thoughts, Jenny turned towards her. They were standing on their own, and for once Jenny appeared to be very serious.

"Listen Dee, I have a lot to apologise for. A couple of years back we were friends and then everything changed, there was a clique here. I wasn't part of it, but I was aware of it. Someone was controlling Janet, making her ruin your life. I should have stopped it, but I didn't have the guts. I hope you can forgive me."

Dee felt shocked. She had assumed that Janet was doing it all herself. And then her heart sank, it sounded as if she was not out of the woods yet.

"Who was this person, and why were they trying to ruin my life?"

"Honestly, I don't know who it is, she is just called 'the boss'. We were all scared of her power, and the threats she made if we tried to be friends with you. I tried to look the other way so I wouldn't be a part of it. I know you are a really nice person, and you don't deserve this!"

"Well, Jenny, thanks so much for being honest with me. Of course I forgive you. I am so glad you told me, it explains a lot of things."

"Maybe you should keep it to yourself, it might cause even more trouble."

Dee knew she couldn't do that. It was something she had to tell the police about, so she made no promises.

"It honestly won't cause more trouble. But whoever this boss is, as far as I am concerned, they have a fight on their hands!"

The bell for assembly went soon after that, and Dee made a mental note to tell her parents when she got home. No more was she going to cope alone. Nathan would report it immediately. It was on her mind for the rest of Tuesday, that behind this apparently nice respectable private school, there lay someone with a secret power which scared pupils into submission. Even with Janet now gone, they could exercise their control again.

It was interfering with her concentration once again and, with less than two weeks left before her exams, it really wasn't helping her at all. She had been so naïve to think her troubles were over, but she was determined to fight against this with all her might. It seemed it was now very personal, and her mother had been used to unsettle her.

When she got home, she spoke to Beth on her mobile before she spoke to her parents. Beth had been the person she had gone to at school and she really missed her not being there, even though it had only been a couple of days. Beth was astounded when she heard what Jenny had told Dee.

"I am amazed to hear this, Dee. I never knew there was a clique and a boss. As much as I like Jenny, do you think she is telling the truth? Poor Janet, maybe she was jealous of you."

This confused Dee even more. She had believed Jenny, her confession had seemed heartfelt. But Beth knew everyone, and was well liked. If there was a boss and a gang, she felt Beth would have known about it.

"OK, fair enough. I do miss you Beth, how are you feeling?"

Beth smiled at the other end of the mobile call. She felt she had been usurped by Jenny. She was jealous of her friendship with Dee, so she felt it was now time to return to school.

"I think my cold is clearing up now, so hopefully tomorrow I'll be back, but of course I don't want you to catch it."

"Don't worry about me, Beth. A cold is the least of my worries."

"Try not to worry about what Jenny said, I don't think it's right. Talking of Jenny, did you know she has a bit of a crush on Billy? I saw how she behaved the other day when she was talking to him, you could see it in her eyes."

116

Dee was surprised, she hadn't even realised that Jenny had met up with Billy.

"I had no idea about this. When did she see him?"

"Oh, don't ask me which day? Come to think of it, it must have been Saturday, it was when you were in hospital. I was in Beltinge buying bread at the shop, and they were chatting away outside the store. Maybe he likes her, too."

When Dee came off the phone, her next planned move had been to tell Nathan and Lydia, but now she wasn't sure, particularly with Beth not believing it. If Jenny had made it up, it would just cause more trouble. She had not realised that Jenny liked Billy, but then, with his dark Latin looks, was it surprising? Her brother was very handsome, even if he did know it.

Then a thought struck her. Had Jenny reunited with her just so she could go out with Billy? If that had been her idea, it was a waste of time, because she had no influence whatsoever on Billy's life, or his choice of girlfriends. She now realised with a sinking heart, that maybe she couldn't trust Jenny at all.

When she woke up on Wednesday morning after a troubled night, she looked at the time and it was only six o'clock, although very light. She turned over and tried to put her tumbled thoughts into some sort of order, as she didn't really need to get up until about seven thirty. But her brain was whirling, so she went downstairs to get a drink of water.

As she passed the hall and the front door, she noticed the cream envelope on the mat. It had obviously been delivered by hand, as there was no stamp on it. Her name Dee was written in very clumsy and wavy capital letters, so she picked it up. She tore the envelope quickly, and drew out the sheet of paper. The writing inside was also very wavy, as though written by an old person who was having trouble guiding the pen. It simply said: '*I KNOW YOU KILLED JANET*'.

Instead of feeling frightened, Dee felt angry. Jenny was right in this instance. Someone was out to get her, to try and break her, but they were not going to succeed. Forgetting her usual politeness, she ran upstairs and, without knocking first, she burst into Nathan and Lydia's room.

117

"Lydia, Dad, look what someone has sent me."

Nathan rose sleepily out of bed and took the outstretched piece of paper from her, but when he read it he was instantly awake.

"Where did you get this from?"

"From the doormat, Daddy."

"It wasn't there last night. What time did we come to bed, Lydia?"

"Oh, about eleven I think, just after the news finished," said Lydia, also reading it.

"So some nutcase delivered it late last night, or very early this morning, just wait until I show it to the police!" said Nathan angrily.

He went to put a comforting arm round Dee, but she wasn't crying, he could see how angry she was.

"But that is not all, Daddy. Yesterday Jenny told me there had been a gang, she was never a part of it, but she said Janet was controlled by someone called 'the boss'. Somebody was out to get me, they still are, and they used bad mouthing Mummy as a way to upset me."

"Right, well DCI Clarke needs to know all this. I suggest we go and see him before you go to school. I can drop you at school later."

"OK Daddy, but I had better let Beth know, she is coming back today and I have arranged to meet her."

"Dee, I don't think you can tell any of your friends that you are going to the police. Let's face it, you don't know which of them you can trust."

With a sinking heart, Dee realised this was true. Beth and Jenny both had conflicting stories. One of them had told the truth, and she had no idea which one. She wanted to think it was Beth, but she had no proof.

She decided to text Beth and say she was coming into school later, as she had an appointment with Maria. That way nobody would know she had been to the police station. She had refrained from telling Jenny that she was going to pass her information onto the police, luckily.

Alan sat opposite Dee and Nathan, listening to what they had to say. He examined the note, and then sent it away for analysis. He had expected to see Dee in tears, but she was clearly very angry. She told him what Jenny had told her about there being a boss.

"That is very interesting," said Alan. "Usually when bullying goes on there is a leader, and we assumed it was Janet. Maybe I should interview Jenny. She was interviewed with the rest of the class and, at the time, didn't appear to have a motive. But maybe she can tell me more about this boss."

"She said she didn't know who it was," said Dee, doubtfully.

Alan paused, he knew Wendy was making a note of this, and it occurred to him they had concentrated all their efforts on the teenagers, but what about Nathan? He was here now and, although a bit extreme, if he had killed Janet, it would be to protect Dee.

"Nathan, can you tell me what time you got home from work last Friday?"

Nathan smiled, he had been expecting it, and he had nothing to hide, so he felt glad the police were doing their job thoroughly.

"Yes, it was just after five. I had left work at four thirty. It took half an hour to get home, as the traffic out of Canterbury was heavy until I got off the main road and drove home via the Hoath Road."

"And who else was home?"

"Lydia cooking dinner, and Jack in his room playing video games. At that time I thought Dee was also in her room, as she had fallen out with Lydia, but, as you know, she had gone out."

"So, did you go out again?"

"Not until we got the call to say that Dee was in hospital."

"You have an alibi then?"

"Yes, we all do." Nathan was glad of that, because if the police cared to delve back into his youth, they would discover he had been arrested for being in possession of cannabis when he was twenty-two years old. But subsequently meeting Philip, and having the support from him and Isabel, had enabled him to turn his life around. He had been given chances to get a good education, and a well paid job. He was nothing like the person he had been then, but the police were always naturally suspicious, and he understood that they had to be.

There was a knock at the door, and Gary entered the room. "There are no fingerprints on that note except ours, sir. We have matched up Dee's and Nathan's as well as yours. Judging by the spidery writing, it would seem the person wrote it with gloves on."

119

"Now that's a shame. We took all the prints of every girl in the class. Thanks, Gary."

Gary left the room, and Alan decided their next move was to interview Jenny. Like all the other girls, she had been interviewed at school on Saturday, but he needed to try and find out more about this boss person she had mentioned. He spoke to Dee and Nathan.

"Thanks for coming in. If we find out any more, we will let you know."

Nathan stood up and thanked him, then turning to Dee he spoke: "Come on, I will run you to school, and not a word of where we have been to anyone."

Chapter Fourteen

Alan knocked on the door of the house where Jenny lived. He had decided not to go to the school. He wanted to interview her away from the school, so nobody else knew. Wendy stood next to him with her pen and notebook in her hand. They had waited until five o'clock, to give her a chance to get home from school.

The door was opened by a girl whom he guessed to be about the same age as Dee, she had auburn hair with golden lights in it from the sun, and it was tied back into a ponytail. They were both in plain clothes, and she gave them a welcoming smile.

"Good afternoon. Are you Jenny Latimer?"

"Yes, have you come to see Mum?"

A lady with the same colour hair could be seen hovering behind her, also smiling. They were both stockily built with pleasant faces.

"No, I am DCI Alan Clarke, and this is WPC Wendy Stuart. We wanted to speak to you about the recent events on Reculver beach."

Jenny couldn't help wondering if this visit was because of what she had said to Dee. She had not been on the bus this morning, and had come into school later.

"Come in, we don't need to do this on the doorstep," said Jenny's mother.

They were ushered into a lounge area with sofas, and offered a cup of tea.

f

"No thank you, we won't take up much of your time," said Wendy, conscious of the fact that Alan would want to get it done as quickly as possible so he could get back to Whitstable.

Jenny didn't feel at all worried about being interviewed. She had been interviewed along with the rest of her class on Saturday, and her fingerprints taken, so this could only be about 'the boss'. Alan's next words confirmed it.

"I understand you told Dee that there was a gang at your school, and Janet was being controlled, is that right?"

"Yes, but they seem to have stopped now Janet is not around."

"So tell me, who is this boss?" Alan stared intently at Jenny, but she held his gaze confidently.

"I truly don't know, as I told Dee. I was not comfortable with the clique. I was not a part of it, so I didn't try to find out."

"But somebody must have told you there was a boss."

"No, I just saw nasty posts on Dee's page on Facebook from 'the boss' and, when she found out, she deleted the account. I don't think she connected 'the boss' with Janet; she thought it was someone else."

"Beth has said she knows nothing about there being a boss."

"She probably doesn't. Beth is a sweet person, who would never get involved with anything nasty. Everyone loves Beth."

"And the day Janet died, you told our officers you were out walking your dog?"

"Yes, but in the other direction. I walked to Tankerton and back. It was a lovely evening."

"Can anyone confirm meeting you?"

At this point Jenny's mother intervened. "Jenny walks Rex every day after school. She gets home at six, has her dinner, and then does her homework."

Alan scrutinised their faces. Her mother was her alibi, but would she have known which direction Jenny had walked? He suddenly realised the dog was absent. There had been no barking when they knocked at the door, and no sign of a dog now.

"Where is your dog Rex?"

Jenny's face took on a look of concern. "He is at the vet, and we are waiting for a phone call so we can pick him up. Mum took him in this morning because he had to have a small operation to remove a lump on his back."

Saying this had clearly disturbed her, as her mother put her arm round Jenny, and said comfortingly, "He will be fine, it's more than likely benign, try not to worry."

"Sorry to hear that," said Alan awkwardly. "We won't take up any more of your time."

Jenny's mother saw them out. As she opened the door she looked back, and then spoke softly: "Rex is her life. She loves him so much that if anything happened to him, I really don't know what she would do. I think he is more important to her than all of her friends."

Alan paused on the doorstep. "During this week she became friends with Dee again, did this surprise you?"

"Not at all, she kept out of all the clique business at school, and she always liked Dee, and didn't approve of the way Janet had treated her."

"She told you about that then."

"She tells me everything, we are very close. Her father died three years ago, so it's just us and Rex now."

"I see, does she show any interest in boys?"

"Well, she hasn't told me about that! Why do you ask?"

"Is it possible that she likes Billy Hopkins, do you think?"

"Dee's half brother? Whoever told you that? It's nonsense."

Alan dodged the question, and moved off the step.

"Thanks for your help, Mrs Latimer, we have to check out everything."

"I do hope Rex is better soon," added Wendy, as they stepped onto the path.

The door was closed on them, and they got into Alan's car. Neither spoke for a moment, and then Alan put the car into gear and drove towards Tankerton along the seafront, past the amusements and pitch and putt. He then ended the silence.

"What did you think of Jenny?"

Wendy was thoughtful. "Maybe a girl who prefers dogs to people. She clearly loves Rex, and did not appear to show any signs of guilt."

"Do you think her resuming a past friendship with Dee is for any other ulterior motive?"

"Her mother seemed to think she felt uncomfortable about Dee being picked on. But even if she does like Billy, it doesn't mean she would kill Janet, that's a bit extreme, isn't it?"

Alan sighed. "Well, you know, Wendy, sometimes we have to explore the extreme, but to me she doesn't seem to have it in her. I hope my gut feeling is right."

Before long they had reached The Marine Hotel. Alan dropped Wendy off, and drove towards Whitstable. He glanced at his watch. It was now six o'clock. He parked the car, and went towards the front door. Zoe saw him coming and opened the door, and he hugged her. He could hear Adam fussing in the background.

"Mum's holding him, but I will have to take over, otherwise she can't do dinner," said Zoe, worriedly.

"It's OK, it's my turn," said Alan soothingly. Fussy or not, he couldn't wait to see him. Family life was such a welcome diversion from a murder inquiry. He walked into the room adjoining the kitchen, where Ruth was walking up and down trying to placate her grandson.

"Let me give you a break," he said, holding out his arms. Ruth surrendered Adam to him, but not without protesting that she didn't mind at all.

"Mum, Alan hasn't seen him all day," Zoe reminded her.

"I know," Ruth blushed, "upset or not he is gorgeous, it's so lovely that you have brought him to stay with us, but I don't want to be an interfering mother-in-law."

"You are not," said Alan, walking up and down with Adam. And to his delight, Adam stopped crying, and fixed his wide blue eyes on him.

He took Adam through the kitchen, and walked around the garden with him whilst the women continued to prepare dinner. He showed his son the tall shrubs and colourful flowers whilst talking soothingly to him.

His thoughts returned to the teenagers that had been interviewed that week. It was a sobering thought that one of them might have committed this murder. One day Adam would be a teenager, and he vowed to himself that he would do his best to instill the right values inside him as he grew up, because he could imagine what heartbreak parents would go through if their child had committed murder. He hugged his son closer to him; being a dad had made him more sensitive, and he knew it, he was now a family man.

Nathan had been hoping that the police would be able to find out who had sent that offending note to Dee. He was filled with anger that she was still being victimised. He had expected her to take it badly, but she just seemed very angry about it. It hadn't had the same wounding effect as the vile taunts about her mother. He voiced his feelings to Lydia as they lay in bed that night.

"Our poor little Dee, it's not right that this all carries on, is it?"

"I know she has been through a lot," agreed Lydia, "but she is proving to be very resilient."

"Lydia, we have never mentioned this since the day we discovered Sadie's diaries in that black box, and we made sure no one would ever read them by burning them, but I must mention it now. We both know that Sadie was mentally very ill, even though she was an excellent mother to Dee. It seems to stem back to when she was a teenager and had that abortion, and Isabel didn't realise how much she was suffering so failed to give her the right support. She had untreated mental illness, and it turned her into a killer. You and I are the only people to know that because of reading her confessions, and we both decided it would cause nothing other than profound grief to tell Isabel, Philip and Dee."

"We did," agreed Lydia, "and I still stand by that. You didn't find out what Sadie had done until a year after her death. Dee worshipped her mother, and doesn't need to know such things, and as for Philip and Isabel, they have suffered enough by losing both of their children. If you shared that knowledge with the police, they would assume that Dee had inherited her mother's madness, and it might even be enough to convict her of killing Janet because of circumstantial evidence. You and I both know that Dee is the gentlest girl, and could not have done it. Sharing Sadie's past would not benefit anyone. It's our secret, and must always remain between us."

"But what about Billy? I see some of his mother's traits in him. It would crucify Philip and Isabel if he had done it."

125

"I know it would. Billy doesn't do himself any favours with his attitude, but all we can do is let the police do their job, and find out who it was."

Nathan turned over and put his arms round Lydia, content in the knowledge that they were both reading from the same page.

"You are my one piece of sanity in this crazy world, and I love you," he said, stroking her forehead gently. Then he fell asleep.

Chapter Fifteen

"I think it might be a good idea to go and interview the Philpotts. We can try and find out what sort of girl Janet was."

"Yes sir, it might give us some insight as to why she wasn't popular as well."

It wasn't the first time that Alan had thought about interviewing them. They had been interviewed by the local police when Janet's death was discovered, and news was they were very grief-stricken, so Alan had put off doing a follow-up until now.

They lived in a bungalow in Beltinge, which was quite easy to find. It was just a small village with a parade of shops along the main street, and a few roads leading off. The Philpotts lived in Terminus Drive, which stretched down from a solicitor's office on the corner, next to two convenience stores. The bungalow was halfway down, it had a small front garden, with a path up to the front door, and shrubs growing either side.

The bungalow looked as if it had been freshly painted; it was big, with a double garage next to it. All the outside paving looked new, and the front garden was immaculate. It looked as though somebody had tended it with care. They rang the doorbell, and then waited for a response.

Alan was expecting Janet's mother to be a middle-aged woman of around forty or fifty, but the woman who opened the door looked ageless. She had bleached blonde hair, neatly dressed on top of her head, was very slim, and was wearing what looked like very expensive clothes. Her silk blouse was loose, and her white slacks fitted her slim frame tightly. She was also wearing white stiletto heels. In his mind, she looked more like an older sister than Janet's mother, and she certainly didn't look as if she was grieving. But he chided himself; maybe that wasn't fair as people grieved in different ways, maybe dressing up made her feel better. Nevertheless, she didn't fit in with any preconceived ideas he had about Janet's mother.

"Good afternoon. Mrs Philpott, I believe?"

She nodded her assent, so Alan continued: "I am DCI Alan Clarke, and this is WPC Wendy Stuart. We were very sorry to hear about your daughter Janet. I wonder if we could come in and speak to you?"

At his words, her demeanour changed completely, her face showed pain and her body seemed to have lost its uprightness, her shoulders hunched forward, and without a word, she held the door wider for them to enter.

"Who is it, Sophie?" A man about mid-forties, wearing a city suit with sandy hair and a moustache, stood inside the hallway. To Alan, they both looked out of place in this seaside town, they looked as though they would fit in better in London.

Sophie's voice was hardly more than a whisper. "Police, they want to talk about Janet."

"Never mind talking about her, find out who killed her!"

"Walter, that is not their fault, give them a chance," she said leading them into a lounge which overlooked a very pretty back garden, as lovingly tended as the front. It had a decking area with furniture and a barbecue, and below there were colourful flower beds all round.

"Your garden is beautiful," said Wendy. In fact the whole bungalow was immaculate; the cream fitted carpets and gleaming furniture, with elegant velvet curtains giving it an air of luxury.

"Thank you, I will tell our gardener," said Walter, with an air of sarcasm about him, which made Alan realise that this interview was going to be difficult.

"Walter works in the city, as I do too sometimes. He only comes home at weekends," explained Sophie. She spoke quietly, as though her thoughts were elsewhere.

128

"Yes, our main home is up there. This is our weekend retreat."

Alan was surprised. He wondered why Janet had been at school in Canterbury if their main home was in London. He decided to find out.

"The reason why we are here is to try and find out more about Janet, and if you can think of any reason why anyone would want to harm her."

He had tried to phrase his words carefully, but it didn't stop Sophie from sobbing. She sat down on the sofa and buried her head in her hands.

"If we could have the time back again it would be different; we failed her!"

"Whatever do you mean?" asked Alan, as Sophie continued to sob.

Wendy moved to comfort her, offering her a box of tissues from the table, and asking her if she wanted a drink. Walter then took over the conversation.

"Janet was our only child. We are both career minded, and had not planned for any children. Sophie runs a model agency, and I work in the city, so being up there was always best for us. We bought this as a weekend retreat and holiday home."

"So why did Janet go to school in Canterbury, if you were mostly up in London?"

"Two years ago, she asked me if she could change schools and live here. We have a housekeeper who used to sleep over with Janet when we were in London."

This sounded like an appalling situation to Alan, to imagine that they would even think of leaving their daughter in a holiday home while they were in London. His next words were spoken coldly.

"So you left your housekeeper to bring your daughter up, and you both continued to run your businesses in London?"

"If only we could have known that this would happen. To have the time back again, we would be different," sobbed Sophie, and Walter just stood there woodenly, not making any attempt to comfort her.

"So how much do you know about your daughter? Did you know she was taunting Dee?"

129

Walter took over, as Sophie was still crying. She seemed inconsolable, and Wendy was doing her best to comfort her.

"We knew none of this, and we are very sorry. We didn't know about Billy, or that she was pregnant. Maybe if we had been around a bit more she might still be alive."

"Did she ever say who her friends were? Did she like the other girls in her class?" continued Alan, but it seemed to him they knew nothing about their own daughter. No wonder they felt so guilty.

"Janet didn't have a lot of friends. We moved her here from the London school because she was teased. Teenage girls can be very cruel to one another. Maybe this is why she did the same to Dee. I am not defending her, I know it was wrong, but obviously she didn't want to go through it again."

"So do you think someone might have been controlling her?"

Walter became very thoughtful. "Yes, I do. Janet didn't have a particularly strong character. I think she could have been led."

"What about your housekeeper, was she close to Janet?"

"I think she was, she was very upset at the news. But you can ask her yourself. Her name is Ava Williams, and she lives in Bishopstone Lane, just up the road from here. She is a widow, so was always happy to stay over with Janet."

"OK, thank you. I am sorry that we had to descend on you at such a difficult time," said Alan. It didn't look as if they could be much more help with his inquiries.

"Oh, just one more thing, where were you both on the day that Janet died? You said this was your weekend home."

Sophie spoke in a wavering voice, "Yes we were travelling home here. The train arrived at Herne Bay at seven thirty, then we got into the car, which was parked in a side road a short walk from the station, and we got back about seven forty-five. It wasn't unusual for Janet to be out at that time, so we didn't realise anything was wrong until they came to tell us they had found her and traced us." She was visibly upset at reliving it, but she carried on.

"We wanted to think it was an accident, that no one would want to harm our daughter; she was just a young teenager. But we were told she had been hit over the back of her head with a rock."

"Yes. I am afraid that is true."

"So you can understand that we now want to sell up and go back to London. And we hope you can find whoever did this terrible act to our Janet."

"We will certainly do our best, and we are very sorry for your loss," said Alan.

They were both silent as they got in the car. It had been a distressing meeting, which was why Alan had waited for a week. Now he wanted to hear what Ava Williams had to say about Janet. He drove past the shops, and round the sharp bend, Walter had said Bishopstone Lane was the fourth turning on the left.

"What is the number of her house?" he asked.

"It's not a number, it's called Field View. Walter says it overlooks fields and in the distance you can spot the local church."

"There it is."

It was a small modest semi-detached bungalow. There was a grass area and a bench out the front, sitting on it enjoying the sunshine was a lady who was probably mid-fifties, with grey hair. She stood to greet them as they approached the gate.

"Good afternoon, we are looking for Mrs Ava Williams."

"Yes, that is me, but who are you?"

Alan showed her his ID, realising they had confused her because they were in plain clothes. She was of slight build, but she moved quickly and energetically.

"Come into the house. We don't need to talk out here."

They followed her inside. It was a small bungalow, but in pristine condition. She led them through her kitchen into a conservatory, which overlooked a tiny garden with pots of colourful flowers outside on the terrace. The kitchen looked as if she had just cleaned it; all the unit tops were sparkling and the floor shone too.

"Can I offer you a drink?" she said, waving towards her kettle. "I have been spring cleaning my kitchen, and worked up quite a thirst. I was just taking five minutes break when you arrived."

"A cold drink would be nice, water is fine," said Alan, who was feeling hot and wishing he could wear a tee shirt to work.

"Water is fine for me, too," said Wendy.

Ava made them all some iced water, adding a slice of lemon to it, and they sat down to drink. She spoke before Alan did.

131

"I suppose you are here about Janet. I still can't quite believe it."

"It's tragic. We have just been to see her parents, but it seems you spent more time with Janet than they did, and we wanted to know more about her."

"I suppose her mother was shedding crocodile tears. She's a right actress that one!" said Ava. Her mouth was twisted and she looked angry.

"You didn't like them, and yet you worked for them," said Alan pointedly.

"I used to work for them in London. Then my husband died, and they said they had a holiday home at Herne Bay, so I decided to come here. Janet didn't like it in London, she was picked on at school because she suffered with acne."

"So she asked to transfer to a school here."

"Yes, and I really like it here, but had no idea they would spend most of their time in London. They said they are selling up now. I guess it's too quiet for the likes of them."

"Well, I can understand why they don't like it now," pointed out Wendy.

Alan continued with his questioning. "So you spent quite a bit of time with Janet."

"Yes, I did, poor girl. It was like she didn't have any parents. All they were interested in was making money. They never wanted a child in the first place."

"Did that upset Janet?"

"She never said. She was used to it, but she seemed to be a loner, and never brought home any friends."

"Did you know about Billy?"

"Well, she didn't tell me. But the day she went to meet him, she took a lot of trouble putting on make-up, so I thought she must have been doing it to impress someone."

"So you were here that day, then?"

"Only until she went. They were coming here for the weekend. I went home just after she left. She said she was going for a walk to Reculver."

"And you live alone here?"

"I do, except for Milly, my black cat."

"Right," Alan was thoughtful. She didn't have an alibi, but he couldn't see she would have had a motive either.

"One last thing. Did you find Janet hard to get along with?"

"On the contrary, she was a quiet girl, and she was very deep. I could never say I was close to her, but that was their fault, they never showed her any love!" she said bitterly.

"You really don't like her parents."

Ava blushed, realising how harsh she sounded. "I did like them, but I never approved of the way they stayed in London when Janet was here. I stayed on for her sake really, and now she has gone."

This time Wendy intervened. "Don't judge them too harshly. After all, the suffering they are experiencing now makes them realise the mistakes they made."

"I know, but I am not going back to London with them. I have made a life here, and I like it. It won't be hard for them to find another housekeeper."

"Thanks very much for your time. We will be off now," said Alan.

Ricky was feeling quite restless now. He had been in England for a week doing his best to support Billy. Thankfully Billy had not been arrested, but he had been told not to leave the country. Ricky had taken time off for this visit, but he knew the FBI would not be keen on him being away for too long.

Philip and Isabel had insisted he move into their home whilst he was there, so he had left his room at The Premier Inn to join them. Between them they had hoped that their continued support would help Billy.

Philip had explained that once this was all over, he was hoping to finance Billy's further education in England by paying for his college fees. He knew that Jill and Simon could not afford to do this, and he was hoping by the time Billy had completed the course, not only would he have matured, but he also might have some idea about what he wanted to do as a career.

Ricky was very impressed by this. Billy was so lucky to have such caring grandparents, but he doubted that his son appreciated them. Maybe when he was a bit older he wouldn't be so self-centred.

"Philip, that is such an awesome gesture. His computer skills are good, it's something that does hold his interest. So maybe they could develop that at college."

Philip smiled. They had all been on tenterhooks in case Billy was called back in for questioning, but a week had passed and nothing had happened. He guessed that Ricky would probably be needed back at his own work place.

"If you need to go back to the States, we can cover it. I am sure your girls must be missing you."

"As it happens, I am needed back at work. But, of course, I will jump on the next flight and be back if anything else happens. My girls are self-sufficient now, but that doesn't stop them from having fights at times."

"They are important to you as well as Billy. He will have to learn that. We know we spoil him a bit here," said Philip apologetically.

Ricky ignored that, he knew it was in a good cause.

"You and Isabel have been amazing. When he is allowed to travel back, I must make sure that he shows his adoptive parents some appreciation. They are very poor, but they have showered him with love these twenty years past."

"Of course," said Philip. "I have spoken to them by email about Billy going to college here, and they seem grateful and thrilled that he would have this opportunity."

"Yes, they are selfless, decent law abiding people."

"I don't think there is any reason for you all to worry about him. The police here are working hard on the case, so hopefully it won't be too long before he can go home."

Ricky was pleased to hear Philip's positivity. Billy wasn't perfect, he had the selfishness and thoughtlessness of youth, but he had time to grow up, and none of that made him a murderer. He was determined to go home content in the knowledge that Billy had not done this, and would soon be joining him in New York.

"I will get hold of the airlines and sort my ticket. Thank you so much for your hospitality, Philip."

Chapter Sixteen

Dee had decided to go for a walk to collect her muddled thoughts. She knew her parents didn't want her to walk alone, but on this occasion she needed peace and quiet without anyone else to talk to. She knew now that someone was trying to frame her for the murder, and in her mind she believed it was the person who had written that note. They had done it, and they wanted her to take the blame. Instead of making her fearful, it made her angry. She did not deserve this!

She had tried to think of someone in her class who had really disliked Janet, because she was convinced it would be one of them. Normally she didn't have a suspicious mind, and thought the best of everyone, but not any more!

The beach held no fears for her. She was a strong swimmer, and somehow she found her walk taking her towards Bishopstone Glen. As a young girl, this had been her favourite place, first with Alice and then her mother, she had stood on the Fairy bridge as a very young girl, and looked to see if she could see any fairies hiding underneath. It had been a wonderful childhood moment to hang onto, in the same way as her belief at the time that there really was a Father Christmas.

And further up, the cliff that jutted out, which they had named The Headland was where Alice had met her death. But Dee found she no longer feared it. The here and now was the most important thing, and she needed to know, for her own piece of mind, who had killed Janet.

Unfortunately for her it had been very close to where she had collapsed, but since Billy had admitted that he had dragged her unconscious body up the beach, and then went to telephone for help, she could now understand why she had not seen Janet. Neither she nor Billy had been that close to her body, and she could understand that in his panic Billy had not seen Janet either.

She stood on the wooden bridge that spanned the glen, trying to capture the wonderment she had experienced when standing there as a child. It would always be a beautiful place to stand and dream. Because of the amount of dry weather they had experienced lately, the spring which ran below it had almost dried up. This happened every summer, and the gurgle of the fast flowing water could only be heard in the winter when the rain came, as it wended its way along.

Her most powerful memory of Janet was her taunting, although she had now forgiven her for that. After all, she was still living, but poor Janet's life had been cut short much too soon. Which of her two friends could she trust? Jenny, who had insisted that Janet was controlled, but had no more information, or Beth, who had always supported her, and now said it was nonsense. Beth had never heard of a gang. Could it be because Beth was so nice that no one had told her?

Beth was always very kind to everyone, she didn't say a bad word about anyone. With her golden hair still worn in plaits, she had an air of innocence which was so refreshing. Beth rarely wore make-up, unlike the others who were always experimenting. Dee, herself, also liked wearing make-up. With Beth, her beauty shone through and she didn't need make-up.

But all the other girls had been like sheep with no backbone of their own. They had sniggered at Janet's comments, but none of them really spoke to Janet, or stood up to be counted. So it had appeared that Janet had no friends, and the only one who spoke to her was Beth, because she would never have ignored anyone.

It was such a puzzle, all of it. She started to walk across the bridge whilst deep in thought. She was intending to walk closer to the Headland. She reckoned if she made several visits, getting closer each time, she would be able to beat it. This time she was determined not to faint.

A glance at her phone showed the time to be just after six o'clock. No one was about, so she braced herself to make the first steps, and then go home, as dinner would be at seven o'clock. She had asked Beth if she wanted to meet up for a bit, but Beth had explained that today was her mother's birthday, so they were going out for a meal. Dee had never met Beth's mother, nor her father, Beth said they both worked long hours and had to travel to and from London every day.

Beth had been very angry, too, when she heard about the note. "We all know it wasn't you. The police will find out who sent that, don't worry," was her response.

As she reached the end of the bridge, she heard what she thought was a lawnmower in the distance. And then the sound was nearer; it was just across the meadow now, and she realised with a shock that it was a motorbike, which was very surprising, as usually there were never motorbikes around this sleepy little glen.

Before she had time to think, it came straight towards her. She briefly glimpsed a figure dressed entirely in black leather, and wearing a black crash helmet. Her fear rose when she saw the bike accelerating. She had just reached the end of the bridge where the path led up to the car park and the Headland. She instinctively jumped to get out of the way, and her arms waved wildly as she was trying to find something stable to grip.

But the flimsy fence at the side of the bridge, which was there to protect anyone from falling into the stream below, gave way, and she found herself falling backwards, knowing that there was no water to break her fall. As she plunged down, all sorts of thoughts rushed through her mind. Was she meeting her doom?

There was a large tree overhanging the steep incline, and as her arm brushed it, she grabbed it with her fingers, using all her strength to hang on. The figure on the motorbike looked at her suspended by just her arms to stop her from plunging down, but how long could she hang on?

"Please help me," she begged. Surely they hadn't meant to do this? But the figure came over and looked at her, emitted a hollow mocking laugh from inside the crash helmet, then got on the motorbike and rode away.

137

Dee's arms were aching, and she knew she couldn't hang on for long. She was praying with all her heart that someone would come and help, because she didn't want to die.

Jack hadn't confided in anyone, but he really did like Jenny. Up until recently, he had not had the slightest interest in girls. But when he met Jenny going to school with Dee, he had been on his bike, whilst they were standing at the bus stop, a feeling came over him that he had never experienced before. Was it her auburn hair that had golden lights in it, the freckles on her nose, or the smile she gave him which lit up her whole face?

He knew he'd got it bad because, when he tried to sleep at night, she dominated his thoughts. As if that wasn't enough, he felt a strange feeling in his stomach which robbed him of his normal appetite.

The sad part about it was she didn't have a clue about how he felt, and he was too scared to tell her. She only had eyes for her dog Rex; although Jack loved him too, he was such a lovely dog. He had heard friends at school boasting about how they had got it on with girls, but he never had, up until now passing exams had been paramount in his mind.

But he knew that even if he had become Jenny's boyfriend, no way would he boast about it to others, it would be far too precious and special to share. With his revision now done, and exams just a short time away, his normally focused mind was full of Jenny.

Once he had found out she had a dog, and she took him out every evening after school, it was easy enough to hang about until she came along. One day she had actually invited him to accompany her. They had walked along to Reculver, and she had told him it was her favourite walk. He had so enjoyed her company. That outing felt really special to him, so special that he didn't tell a soul, not even Dee, he just hugged the secret deep inside him.

He summoned all of his courage and went to knock at her house today, to find out if she was taking Rex out. His heart ached for her when she told him Rex was at the vet. Rex was only three years old, but he was having a lump removed from his back. She told him that

138

her mother had been trying to reassure her that he would be fine, and he said he hoped so too. He realised just how much her dog meant to her.

Jack asked her to text him later and let him know how Rex was doing when he came back from the vet. He left her house, and now he was at a loss. He didn't usually go for walks, he rode his bike everywhere. But this had been a way to share a common interest with Jenny.

When he arrived home, he wasn't in the mood to play any computer games. He felt at a loose end, so he stood outside the kitchen window debating what to do next.

Lydia spotted him outside, and called through the kitchen window. "Oh, there you are Jack, are you off out on your bike? Dee is also out somewhere. I hope she's not on her own. Dinner will be at seven."

A bike ride seemed a good idea to Jack. He could pedal all that disappointment out of his system. He decided to cycle to Reculver and back, it was a great ride along the promenade.

"Yes, I'll be back by seven," he promised her, wheeling his bike out of the garage.

Lydia watched him pedal away. She had noticed that something wasn't quite right with Jack, he usually showed great enthusiasm when food was mentioned. She did hope he wasn't coming down with a nasty bug.

Jack cycled quickly along the promenade, which came to an end at Bishopstone beach. There were a few people out walking their dogs. Some were on the beach throwing balls, and he felt a pang of disappointment that he wasn't doing the same with Jenny. Going out with her was fun. She had a great sense of humour, and he had found her very easy company.

When he had gone out with her before, Jenny had thrown sticks into the water, and Rex had valiantly swum out to retrieve them and bring them back. He really hoped that Rex would be better soon, and back on the beach having fun.

He walked his bike up the slope and past the car park, then he proceeded to cross the wooden bridge which spanned the glen. During his ride along the promenade he thought he had spotted Dee walking on the beach, but it was hard to be sure from a distance. He knew Lydia and Nathan were not that keen on her walking around on her own after the recent events, although at this time of the year it stayed light until late.

The girl he had seen had dark hair, but she was alone. So it may have been Dee, but he wasn't going to grass her up if she had come on her own. Lydia had already said that she hoped Dee was with someone.

He picked up the cycle path again in Manor Road, and cycled to the top where it continued along the downs to Reculver. When he got to Reculver, he cycled past the tourist office and the museum, which were both now closed, and past the children's playground. He noticed two young girls on the swings, shouting excitedly at an older girl to push them, both wanting to go higher than the other.

The ice cream shop was now about to close, as it was nearly five thirty, but the lady didn't mind serving him with a ninety-nine cone. He sat down on the grass to eat it, idly watching the girls on the swings. When he had finished, he decided it was time that he went home. He had no reason to hurry, as he would be in plenty of time for dinner.

He continued along the downs. The first part was downhill, but after that he had to put some more energy into his cycling to get up the hill. He came out at the top of Manor Road, and cycled back down it until he reached the entrance to Bishopstone Glen.

He dismounted when he got close to the bridge, remembering there was a notice strictly forbidding cyclists to ride over it; the alternative was to go the long way, and follow the path that ran parallel to the meadow, but he chose the shorter route.

He could see there was good reason for the notice, as it was a narrow bridge, and it would be so easy to bump into someone and injure them whilst crossing. But as he got closer to the bridge, he had the shock of his life, he could hear a voice yelling out in deep distress.

"Please help me, I can't hold on!" and that voice sounded just like Dee. Then, just as he wheeled his bike onto the bridge, he saw her, clinging desperately to a branch of an overhanging tree, and suspended over the steep incline of fallen cliffs and rocks.

He did not hesitate for a moment. Slinging his bike onto the ground, he lay down and leaned over as far as he could. "Grip my arm, Dee, I won't let you fall!"

Dee desperately tried to reach him, and then they both heard the branch cracking. In that moment she thought her life was over. She could see Jack, so near, and yet so far, but she could do no more to help herself.

But Jack wasn't giving up on her. He pushed his bike over the top of the chasm, holding the back end of it.

"Grab the wheel, Dee, I will haul you up."

She could feel her arms losing strength, so she prayed as she lunged towards the bike wheel, grabbing the spokes and tyre just as the branch finally snapped and fell down to the depths below.

Jack used every bit of his strength to haul the bike up. He had lost his glasses, but he didn't care, they had dropped into the depths of the chasm, and Dee's face became blurry.

"Don't let go, Dee, and don't speak. Save your strength!" he gasped.

Little by little, his bike, with Dee desperately clinging onto the end of it, came over the precipice. He gave one final haul, and she was at the top, sprawled on her stomach, with bits of broken fencing hanging from her body. He had fallen back with the effort, but heedless of any cuts and bruises that he had sustained, he rushed over to help her up.

"Dee, what on earth were you doing down there? What happened?" he said, noticing the broken fence. Surely she hadn't just fallen down.

Dee couldn't stop shaking, and now the tears came, tears of relief that she had been saved. She had felt that death had been staring her right in the face. Her words were almost incoherent, punctuated by gulps and sobs.

"S-s-someone tried to kill me. A man on a motorbike tried to run me down."

"What, are you sure?"

Jack glanced around him at the peaceful glen, bringing a motorbike round here would be difficult. The paths were bumpy and narrow, and it was not near to the road. A lady was strolling past

141

with her dog, and she looked over at Dee sitting on the ground and clearly in distress.

"Are you OK? Shall I call an ambulance?"

Now that the shock was subsiding, Dee felt angry, and her words were firm.

"No need, I am OK now. Did you see the motorbike? He tried to kill me!"

The woman looked startled and, to Dee's frustration, she shook her head.

"No, I am the only person around here right now. I expect everyone is having their tea. Motorbikes don't come up here."

"I'll phone Dad," said Jack. He could see that Dee really believed that someone had tried to harm her, but it seemed unbelievable. Dad would know what to do.

"Jack, you have saved my life, and in doing so lost your glasses," said Dee with feeling.

As she felt she could do no more to help, the woman said goodbye and walked off.

Jack was by now on his mobile, ringing Nathan, who had arrived home from work. He explained exactly where they were, and Nathan suggested if Dee could walk, they should go and sit in the picnic area on the wooden seats in the glen. He would then bring the car down to the white gates, park outside, and collect them from there.

Jack helped Dee up from the ground, and brushed away all the bits of branches that were clinging to her clothes. Her hands had cuts on them, but apart from that she was shocked more than anything. She insisted that she could walk, so Jack picked up his bike, which was also covered in twigs, and walked just behind her. As they were crossing towards the seats, Dee kept insisting there had been a man on a motorbike. So he realised that, in her mind, that was how she had come to grief.

Dee knew that when Nathan arrived she could well be in for a rollicking for going out walking alone. But by the time he arrived, her fear had been replaced by anger and frustration because the woman hadn't seemed to believe her. Once again, she described exactly what happened to her, insisting it had been a man, all dressed in black, including his crash helmet, on a motorbike. She also pointed out there was no doubt it had been a deliberate act, as he had done nothing to help her, and laughed before riding off.

Nathan chided her gently for walking alone. But he could see how determined she was, so he suggested that they contact the police, and then it could be investigated. Somebody in this area must have heard, or even seen, the motorbike.

"It's nearly seven o'clock, and the station will now be closed, but I will ring Alan Clarke first thing tomorrow," he promised her.

"Thanks Dad," said Dee, at least he believed her. She felt Jack didn't, and now she felt like her mind was trying to play tricks on her. Why was she the only person to see the man on the motorbike? As unlikely as it sounded, that person had driven her off the end of the bridge, and she had almost met her doom. Thank goodness Jack had been around for her!

Chapter Seventeen

Zoe had settled into a very enjoyable way of life in Whitstable during the past week or so. Having her parents around whilst Alan was at work was a real bonus, as they both enjoyed holding and interacting with Adam. Her mother often changed his nappies, so Zoe could have a few precious minutes to herself.

Gerald was very good with him, too. He liked taking him out in his buggy, and showing his grandson off. Zoe couldn't help smiling to herself, as she hadn't remembered him taking the same interest in her and her sister when they were young, but now he had become a modern man. Her mum had always said he didn't handle them very often when they were babies, as he thought they might break. However, he had no such problems with Adam.

After a few days he had suggested that Zoe and Ruth might enjoy a shopping trip to Canterbury, it being so close, and he could take care of Adam whilst they went. Zoe was hesitant at first, but lately she had been expressing some of her milk. Alan had suggested that, so if Adam woke up in the night for a feed, he could take a turn as well. This meant Adam was learning to drink from a bottle as well as the breast, so Gerald could feed him if he woke up early for a feed whilst they were still out.

Zoe had always been keen to visit Canterbury Cathedral and soak up all the history inside. Her figure was still not back to normal, so she wasn't interested in buying anything new for her wardrobe, but it would be really nice to go shopping with her mother. She couldn't remember the last time that had happened. Gerald promised he would keep in touch by text and with photos, as he had just mastered how to do it.

So they set off about eleven o'clock. Adam had just had a really good feed, and he was putting on weight nicely, with a healthy glow in his cheeks, which put Zoe's mind at rest. Life in Whitstable was really suiting them all.

Alan was totally immersed in his case, without much time off, which she had expected. So spending time with her parents, and knowing how much they were enjoying their grandson, was lovely. Zoe got herself ready to go, feeling excited at the prospect of enjoying a little time to herself.

Ruth drove into Canterbury, taking the picturesque route along the Hoath Road. She was used to negotiating the narrow lanes. When they reached the level crossing, it was the usual hustle and bustle, but having got to know the area, she knew where to park, and she had chosen inside a multi-storey car park.

The first place they visited was the Cathedral. They walked across the cobblestones to the entrance, and Zoe marvelled at the architecture, imagining coaches and horses from centuries past coming down the narrow streets.

A man stood at the gateway before they entered. The whole area was flanked with groups of students of all ages, chattering. They came from many different countries, and were talking very excitedly in many different languages.

After a while, a guide appeared to show the students around, so Ruth and Zoe went too, realising that they would learn more about it when he spoke. As they approached the steps leading up to the cathedral, he explained how Thomas Becket had been murdered in 1170 with a single blow from a sword on a cold December evening. He then moved inside, pointing out the beauty of the stained glass windows.

Zoe was transported into a medieval world; the pulpit and the ancient pews captured her eye. She found the beauty of the cathedral and its grounds breathtaking, and when they emerged into the light again she felt so glad to have experienced it.

She came back to the 21st century when she received a text from

g

Gerald to say that Adam was sleeping peacefully, accompanied by a picture of him with a very contented look on his face, and his arms pointing upwards, which Zoe knew always meant he was in a deep sleep. Now she was enjoying her trip out even more.

They walked up the narrow cobbled streets, which were a feature of the city, with shops built on either side. It was lunchtime now, so Ruth suggested getting something to eat.

"We could either pop into a restaurant; there is one in particular I have in mind, it's sixteenth century, and right outside the window it has the famous Ducking Chair, it's where the high street meets the River Stour. . . "

"That sounds fun, I can take some photos," said Zoe

". . .or we could get fish and chips, and eat them in the gardens which start at Westgate Towers, and stretch right up to the other end of the town. It's so pretty with the river running through, and the flowers have been planted with great attention to detail. The colours are amazing. I love to sit on a bench and drink it all in," said Ruth, proudly showing off the beautiful city.

"Mum, you sound like someone from the tourist office," said Zoe mischievously, her eyes twinkling. But I do agree with you, it's lovely."

"I have a good idea. Let's walk down and take pictures of the Ducking Chair, and then go and get fish and chips and enjoy the gardens and the river," said Zoe.

"Why not?" agreed Ruth. She was enjoying this time with Zoe so much that she secretly wished it would never end, but she knew that once Alan solved the case they would be off again. So she had to make the most of it now.

They strolled down the cobbled street towards the sixteenth century restaurant. It was already full of people, so Zoe took her phone out and got some shots from various angles.

"Look at the people going in, Mum, I think we made the right decision," she remarked. "I have enough photos now. Let's go and get our lunch."

They found the fish and chip shop, and that too was busy. They queued up to get their fish and chips. It seemed that everywhere in Canterbury was busy, but that was part of the attraction; a place where people of many different nationalities came together to enjoy the experience of the bustling city. They entered the gardens and searched for an empty seat to sit on. Eventually they found a spot by the river, with swans and ducks gliding peacefully by, and they sat on a bench. Zoe had not realised just how picturesque Canterbury was. She was really enjoying her day out.

Alan sat opposite Nathan, Dee and Jack. They had relayed the incident from the evening before to him in full detail. It sounded to him as though Dee had been very lucky that Jack happened to come along that way on his bike. Jack explained about the bridge, and the chasm it covered, and he said it was a long way down to the bottom.

"Can you describe the person on the motorbike?" he asked Dee.

She did not hesitate. "Yes, he was dressed all in black. His crash helmet was black as well, but, of course, I couldn't see his face."

"So you don't know for sure it was a man then, it could have been a woman?"

"I suppose so." Her voice faltered. She had assumed it was a man because of the aggressive way they were driving. You didn't see many women on motorbikes round this area. In fact, she had never seen any before. She almost felt she had imagined it.

"Well, I am glad to see you were not seriously injured. Well done to Jack for saving you!" He turned and smiled at Jack, who now had a new pair of glasses on and grinned back.

"Thank you so much for telling me. What I will do now is send officers out to question some of the people who live around the glen, and maybe we can find out which direction this rider came from."

After they had gone, he put his plan into action. Several of his team were sent out. He needed to know more about this incident before he had a team meeting later to once again go through the suspects. It sounded very much as though someone was out to get Dee. First the note, and now this incident.

It was no great surprise to him to receive a phone call later from a very concerned Nathan, who hadn't wanted to alarm Dee too much in front of her, but now asking what they were going to do about Dee's safety. He assured him he had it in hand, and would discuss it at the meeting later.

Alan and his team met up in the main office after lunch, but it seemed the inquiries had led to nothing. Nobody living near to the glen had seen or heard a motorbike. Alan prepared himself to address his team and share his theories, as that was all he had at the moment with the lack of any real evidence. Pinned on the big board were photos of everyone involved with the case. He started with Dee whilst his theory was fresh in his mind.

"I am going to run through all this again. If you think of anything new, put your hand up and speak. Dee Edwards, sixteen years old, daughter of the late Sadie Morton Brown, resembles her in looks, but appears to be much quieter, naïve, and shows no signs of violence, or having a bad temper. However, this young girl was found very close to the murdered Janet Philpott. It is now known her half-brother Billy Hopkins dragged her unconscious body up the beach, so her claim that she doesn't remember any of it could be true. She has had a traumatic life after witnessing the death of her nanny when she fell off the cliffs at Bishopstone, and then a short time later her mother was killed in a road accident. She had counselling, and appeared to have coped until two years ago."

He paused, all eyes were intent on him so he continued.

"Two years ago Janet joined the school, and started taunting Dee with stories; we don't know whether they are true or not. Dee reacted by displaying difficult behaviour at home. Then Janet is killed, and Dee admits to her family that Janet was goading her."

Wendy put her hand up, and Alan nodded to her.

"Sir, when I check my notes, I find that Nathan Edwards said that Dee confessed to him about the bullying from Janet before local police told them that Janet was dead."

Alan was thoughtful. "Interesting, so if Dee was involved with the killing, and just pretending that she fainted, she already knew Janet was dead, so it was safe for her to talk about it."

He went on. "As we know, Sadie had a history of mental illness, and it's possible Dee may have inherited it. Her life has been full of trauma, so maybe she was pushed into a situation where killing Janet would give her peace. Sometimes people with mental illness can wear two hats. Maybe the part of her brain that controls her conscience couldn't rest, so she sent herself that note accusing herself of killing Janet. Then yesterday, knowing her stepbrother was around, she positioned herself hanging onto a branch so he could rescue her from what she claims to be a man on a motorbike dressed all in black. The only problem is, Jack didn't see or hear him, nor did anyone else living round there. So how can we trust anything that she says?"

Alan looked around him for some sort of reaction to his theory, and he noticed Wendy was busy scanning her notes. There was a murmur of conversation, then Gary spoke up.

"Well sir, I think she may have risked her life by hanging over the edge like that. Why not interview her counsellor? Maybe they could give an insight into Dee's state of mind."

"Could she have worked together with Billy Hopkins? They were both there at the same time?" suggested another officer.

"I am coming onto Billy in a minute. Yes, Gary, I think that is a good idea, although these professional people are always difficult to interview because of their confidentiality clause. Maria appears to be a family friend, visiting Dee at home even though she has a Harley Street practice."

"OK sir, I have noted that for later," said Wendy.

Alan pointed the tip of his pen towards the photograph of Billy. "Billy Hopkins, half-brother to Dee, both sharing the same mother, travels between here and the USA since he has become known to his grandparents following the death of his mother. Also Janet's on/off boyfriend. Didn't show much emotion when told she had died, knew she was pregnant, and admitted to seeing both Janet and Dee on the beach that day. Also admitted that he gave Dee a puff of his cigarette when he saw her and she said she felt faint. It was further down the beach, but we found the marks he made in the sand when he dragged her to the cave entrance where she was found. We also found out he was the person who used the call box in Manor Road to get help for Dee. He has a criminal record in the States for petty theft, and recently I interviewed a man who lodged a complaint against him two years ago for assault, but later he withdrew it. He is known to be violent, with

149

an uncontrollable temper, and has a guilty manner, and was also desperate to leave the UK."

"I am not surprised," remarked Gary. "He definitely sounds suspicious. It could have been an argument, and then he hit her with a rock, not intending to kill her."

"But if he had done it, why move Dee's body up to the scene of the crime? Either to protect her from the tide, or to frame her for the murder," mused Alan. "Could Dee and Billy have actually done this together? I wonder."

He left them to ponder on that, pointing towards the photo of Jenny.

"Now there are twenty-seven girls in Dee's class, they were all interviewed, and it appears that Janet was not popular. They all have an alibi except this one. Jenny Latimer, used to be a friend of Dee until Janet came to the school. But has now become friendly with her again, and insists there was a boss controlling Janet, and all the other girls, and she said she was scared and did not want to be a part of it. All the other girls, including Dee's best friend Beth, have denied this. Apart from that she seems a normal teenager; owns a dog that she walks a lot. She has no real alibi for that day, she said she walked to Tankerton, which is the other direction, and claims not to have met anyone who could verify her alibi for that day, so we only have her word for it."

Wendy put her hand up again. "Maybe that is because they are all scared, sir. She may be telling the truth."

Alan agreed. "That may well be true because we interviewed the housekeeper of the Philpotts, Ava Williams, and she said Janet was a very quiet girl and also deep, Her own alibi was flimsy, she was home alone in her bungalow, but again we can't see what motive she would have had. Walter Philpott said his daughter might have been controlled, as she was not particularly a strong-minded character."

Alan pointed next to the photograph of Beth. She smiled into the camera, and her blue eyes were captivating, her blonde hair in plaits made her look younger than her sixteen years. He explained that she was Dee's closest friend, and was with her before she went to the beach, as they had spent time at the cinema together.

"Dee is her alibi, she saw Beth onto her bus home."

"They could have done it together," suggested Gary.

This time it was Wendy who spoke.

"We interviewed her on the beach at her suggestion, which was a little unusual. She seemed very likeable, and genuinely caring about Dee. The only reservation we had about her was that she didn't want us to go to her house, so we checked the next day to make sure she lived there, and found her home from school and sick."

Alan sat down and allowed his team to discuss the case. It was always good to get other points of view, because sometimes the truth was staring you right in the face, and yet you couldn't see it. They had separated into two groups. After fifteen minutes he spoke again.

"Well guys, what do you think?"

Gary was the first to speak. "Apart from the teenagers you mention, what about the Morton Brown family? They have certainly been through it in the past. Have the parents and grandparents been checked out?"

"Oh yes. Nathan travelled home from work in Canterbury, and was with Lydia until they got the news about Dee being found on the beach. Her step-brother Jack was also there. Isabel and Philip were at home, so they have each other as an alibi, and again no motive, as none of them knew about the bullying until after Janet had been found dead."

"Looks like there are only three possibilities then," said Wendy, "or maybe four; Beth, Dee, Billy or Jenny."

Chapter Eighteen

Maria Firth was fifty years old, and she looked at least a decade younger. Her long dark hair was carefully maintained the same colour; every time the slightest bit of grey showed she went to her hairdressers. She had been divorced for a few years now, and was happily single, as she felt having a man in her life was an added complication.

She had always eaten the right food and kept herself slim, and regular trips to the gym ensured that she stayed that way. Her son and daughter were both grown up now, with their own lives, and she had grandchildren that she enjoyed seeing on a regular basis.

She was enjoying her independence, and she had always loved her job. Trying to help children with their emotional insecurities, and helping them to make sense of the world, was her challenge, and she had grasped it with both hands.

Maria had acted as both counsellor and psychologist to Dee from when she was six years old. Nathan had paid her handsomely for taking the trouble to visit her at home, after explaining he felt his little girl would feel more comfortable in her own familiar surroundings.

It had been a surprise to Maria to discover just how resilient Dee was. She had witnessed her nanny's violent death, closely followed by the death of her adored mother, and for a short time, her naturally sunny and happy-go-lucky nature had been replaced by fear and anxiety. But love always wins through, and Nathan and Lydia made sure she had plenty of that. It had been a joy to see that smile back on her face again, and then her infectious giggle. Dee was a delightful little girl with a heart of gold, and Nathan and Lydia had brought her up to have such nice manners.

Recently Nathan had contacted her again, explaining that Dee had been bullied at school, and the girl who bullied her had been murdered. Apparently lately Dee had been giving her parents a hard time, and now they knew why. This latest happening had fuelled her fear of Bishopstone Glen and the Headland again, so Maria had offered to visit Dee to see if she could help her.

Her biggest shock was when she saw Dee again; she was blossoming into a young woman now, and would be a real beauty. Maria did remember all about Sadie Morton Brown, the woman who was not fit to stand trial, and how she was rehabilitated afterwards. She had certainly been an interesting case, but this was where the similarity to her mother ended.

Dee's greatest attraction was her naïvety, whereas her mother had been streetwise. Dee wasn't aware of her looks, so she was unable to use them in the way that Sadie had. Sadie had used her sultry beauty to captivate and ensnare men. Dee was shy, but she had a determined nature, she was definitely no pushover, and at their recent meeting, she had told Maria very firmly that she intended to conquer her fear of the Headland so she could walk there in peace. It seemed to Maria that Dee was growing up, and finding her way in life, and she reiterated to her that she would always be there to listen if Dee had a problem.

She wasn't that surprised to be contacted by the police, but this time they were coming to her. She had arranged an appointment for midday to enable them time to get to London from Canterbury. She guessed they would want to ask her about Dee's character, because part of her job as a psychologist was to assess the children that came to her for help. Client confidentiality prohibited her from talking about certain things, but she knew she would be able to present a positive picture of Dee to them.

Alan had toyed with the idea of sending someone else to London. He was enjoying being in Canterbury and the surrounding area. Most evenings he arrived back in Whitstable shortly after five, which gave him time to hold Adam, and be a part of things before dinner. Gerald usually poured him a beer, and then they had a walk round the garden, which was nice. Back home in Dulwich, after leaving the railway station, he could spend a couple of hours in a traffic jam just to drive two miles home, and then arrive back to a late dinner. Did he really want to squash amongst the rest of the world in a tube in this hot weather to get to Harley Street?

But in the end curiosity had won, he wanted to meet Maria Firth. She hadn't treated Sadie, but would more than likely remember the case. So if Dee had any of her mother's traits, then Maria would know.

He had told Wendy just to wear plain clothes, as travelling through London by train, and then turning up at Maria's practice, would cause an immense stir. He was wearing casual clothes, light trousers and a short-sleeved open-necked shirt. As it was so warm Wendy had a simple skirt and blouse with sandals on.

They caught the train from Canterbury, and then took the tube. As it wasn't rush hour it was just about bearable, although hot inside the underground train. They walked along Harley Street until they found Maria's practice, with her name outside. She shared it with another person, but it was Maria they wanted to see.

They were not kept waiting for long. As the receptionist showed them into Maria's office, Maria rose to greet them smiling. Alan noted she looked every bit the professional. Her dark hair was dressed neatly on top of her head, and she wore a bluish grey suit with a crisp white blouse. She was an attractive lady, and had obviously looked after herself as her figure was trim and youthful. He guessed her age to be anywhere between forty and fifty, it was hard to tell.

"Good morning, Miss Firth, may we call you Maria? My name is DCI Alan Clarke, and this is my partner WPC Wendy Stuart."

"It's Mrs Firth by the way, and you may certainly call me Maria."

They all shook hands, and sat down. "Would you like a tea or coffee, or even a cold drink?" she asked hospitably.

"Well, it was hot on the tube, so a cold drink would be really nice, just water," suggested Wendy.

Maria pressed the buzzer and requested a jug of iced water and some biscuits. Alan was pleased as breakfast seemed a long time ago. They wouldn't be able to have lunch just yet.

"What can I do for you today?"

Alan explained the whole situation. How Dee couldn't remember being on the beach, and the bullying she had suffered at the hands of Janet. Then the note accusing her of killing Janet, and finally the mysterious figure in black, who had supposedly run her off the bridge, and yet no one, including her step-brother who had rescued her, had heard or seen any of it.

Maria listened carefully, and even made some notes, then she sat back in her chair to consider her words before she spoke.

"I cannot discuss Dee's case with you as you well know."

Alan knew he would have to be tactful here. Sitting before him was a very determined lady, and he had to keep on the right side of her.

"I am not asking you to do that. I just wanted your very valued professional opinion of Dee. As you know, this is a murder case, and this particular young lady has had a very troubled past, through no fault of her own, so I want to understand the sort of person she has become now."

His charm was not lost on Maria, praising her up to get information out of her, but she felt that he did care what happened to Dee, and so did she.

Wendy also spoke. "We find Dee to be very well brought up with polite manners, and she also seems to be very well loved."

"I am going to be very frank with you both. First of all, Alan, I got the impression that when you recounted recent developments, you were not sure if they were true. Is that right?"

Alan felt a bit like he was in front of his headmistress, but he hid it. "I am only too aware of how much trauma Dee has suffered from a very early age, and then the bullying from Janet. . ."

". . .and you wondered if she had snapped and killed Janet, no doubt?"

"As a detective, I have to be suspicious of everyone," he said smoothly, not allowing her stern expression to intimidate him.

"I can't give you an answer about that, only Dee knows. What I can tell you is that during her life, Dee has had to put up with being

155

compared to her mother, and everyone knows that Sadie suffered from mental illness. I have seen nothing to suggest that Dee has inherited her mother's madness."

She paused as the door opened to admit her receptionist with a tray containing a jug of iced water and glasses with slices of lemon in, and a packet of chocolate digestive biscuits.

Maria poured out the water, then handed them their glasses.

"I will have a biscuit, thanks very much," said Alan, eyeing the packet.

"We had a very early breakfast," explained Wendy, taking just one, while Alan took a couple.

Maria resumed speaking whilst they were munching.

"I saw Dee recently, just after Janet died, and by then I knew about the bullying. This was yet another trauma for her to deal with. To be honest, most teenagers who had been through what she has would have had a breakdown by now. But Dee seems to have a quiet strength and determination which helps her to cope with life." She paused to have a sip of water.

"I have no reason to doubt that she is an honest person. I have never seen any signs of uncontrollable temper, or a split personality. In my opinion, if she says she has received a note accusing her of the murder, and has also almost been mown down by a maniac, my impulse would be to believe her. It sounds to me as though she needs some police protection. I don't believe that she is capable of murdering anyone. But remember, this is my opinion, and it's not backed up by any facts, so you need to make your own judgements."

Alan digested her words. She believed in Dee, and he wanted to as well.

"Thanks very much, you have been very helpful," he said. "We won't take up any more of your time."

He was deep in thought on the train going back, and Wendy had by now stored her notes in a big handbag, and was idly looking out of the window, watching the stations going past as the train made its way back to Canterbury. A few people were sitting around them; a man buried in a newspaper, and a young woman who was busy on her mobile phone.

When they arrived at the police station it was three thirty, and not much seemed to be happening. Alan couldn't help thinking fleetingly how nice it would be to leave early, and spend some time with Adam and Zoe. They had worked right through the weekend, and he felt he needed a break. He didn't particularly have to answer to anyone, he was his own boss, and he felt he needed some time to assess the case again before they could move forward.

He addressed Wendy: "I think we can finish early today, would you like to go back to your hotel now?"

Wendy visibly brightened. She was hot from travelling on the train, and it had been hard working all over the weekend too. She had made plans to go shopping, but until now had to put them on hold. Even a couple of hours off now would be nice. There was a parade of very interesting shops at Tankerton, behind her hotel, so she could have a look around. Once Alan was immersed in a case, especially one as puzzling as this one, very little would distract him, so she welcomed this opportunity.

"Thanks boss, I want to do a bit of shopping locally in Tankerton."

Alan realised that maybe he had been a bit too focused on the job. "We won't work all of next weekend. Zoe has been telling me how lovely Canterbury is. She visited the Cathedral with her mum the other day. I want to go back with her myself."

Wendy felt pleased. "That's great, and I have heard it has a fantastic amount of shops there too."

"Yes, you ladies certainly like the shopping. I am interested in it from the historical point of view. They have also rebuilt the Marlowe Theatre, and they stage some great productions there."

"Now that you have ready-made babysitters, you could take Zoe there," pointed out Wendy. She was enjoying being in this area a lot, and her hotel was very comfortable. The only reservation she had was that she was missing her brother Leo who had Asperger Syndrome, and her mother Karen. They were a close family, and ever since she had been kidnapped by the psychopath some eighteen months ago, they had become even closer.

"If we are definitely not working next weekend, then I think Mum and Leo might like to come down. They are very interested in looking round the area."

157

"That would be nice for you, Wendy. I expect they are missing you. I promise you this, even if something happens and I have to work, you can have a free weekend."

Wendy smiled. "Thanks boss, that means a lot." That was good news, so now she could make some arrangements when she spoke to her mother.

She knew how lucky she was to work with such a man as Alan. Fair and honest, and understanding when he needed to be. And he wouldn't put pressure on any of the suspects like some police did. He had his own methods of dealing with cases, and she knew he would solve it. But right now they both had enough to ponder on, and this evening she would go through all the notes she had made, just in case something really was staring her in the face, because even when they were not at work, their minds often were.

Chapter Nineteen

Dee felt quite shaken up for a few days after being confronted by the figure on a motorcycle. But what made it worse was she didn't have any witnesses, which meant after an initial investigation, the police were not taking it seriously.

Jack had seen and heard nothing, but he said he believed her, and so did Nathan. She felt quite clear-headed, she wasn't going mad, but as each day passed she was becoming more and more frustrated, as it was clear to her that somebody out there wanted to get rid of her. It was a scary thought, and in the beginning she had stayed close to home where she felt safe. But then she decided she couldn't wait any longer for the police to solve it, she was going to do her own investigating.

She found herself getting suspicious of everyone. Up until now it had not been in her nature, but the recent happenings had caused her to view everyone in a different way. She could not fail to see that Jack was carrying a torch for Jenny, he had even started to come to school with them on the bus, just so he could get a glimpse of her. Suddenly cycling to school had lost its attraction.

If Jenny had noticed she gave nothing away, but Dee had noticed, and so had Beth. Yet Beth had seemed to think that Jenny was interested in Billy. Dee had not been aware of Jenny going anywhere with Billy, or even coming into contact with him, as his dad had been visiting and they had spent most of that time together.

They all got the No. 7 bus into Canterbury every weekday

morning, and the more Jack showed a softer side to him, the more she worried that Jenny was in some way using him to get to her.

She became fixated that Jenny had some connection with the figure on the motorbike, and as usual she shared her fears with Beth. It was hard for Beth to criticise anyone, she was just too nice, but she listened sympathetically to Dee, and reiterated her belief that Dee had not imagined the incident with the maniac on the motorbike, it had actually happened.

Dee's plan was to get inside Jenny's house. She didn't know what she would find there, but she was determined to look around if she got the opportunity. Her exams were due to start next week, and she didn't know if she was properly focused, but Daddy had been brilliant. He had already told her if she didn't pass, she could take them again. With that pressure now taken off her shoulders, she felt she could cope with the way her life was being turned upside down right now.

After they disembarked from the bus today, she had said goodbye to Beth who had to get another one to Greenhill. Jack was walking just behind them, too shy to walk next to Jenny. It was laughable really, her stepbrother, who usually went everywhere by bike, and until now had never shown the slightest interest in girls, was now firmly under the spell of Jenny. And Dee found this worrying, as she just wasn't sure she could trust Jenny.

She decided that now was the time to put her plan into action.

"Jenny, we have French tomorrow. I wondered if I could come round, then we could test each other."

"Dee, you are much better at French than I am, but why not. I am taking Rex out first. He has recovered well from his operation. I will probably be back home at about five."

"OK, I will come at five then. See you later."

They parted company, it was handy that Jenny only lived round the corner in Sea View Road, and it was walking distance. With Jenny now gone, Jack fell into step next to her.

"Well sis, I was hoping she might ask me to go on another walk with her, but I don't think she even notices me," he said gloomily.

"Maybe after our exams, when we have more free time, then she will notice you. Jack, you have got it bad!" laughed Dee, doing her

160

best to keep the conversation light. Every fibre of her being was shouting at her to warn Jack about Jenny, but she knew he wouldn't listen. If she was in his place, she would be the same, people telling you that someone wasn't nice when you liked them, or warning you not to get involved, was as if they thought you didn't have a mind of your own. It wasn't even as if she had any evidence, only a hunch. She hadn't even told Beth she was going to Jenny's tonight. It had been an impulse decision.

When they arrived home, she stopped briefly for a cold drink and a packet of crisps. There was an enticing aroma coming from the kitchen where Lydia was busy peeling potatoes.

"Mm, Lydia, that does smell great," remarked Dee. "What time is dinner?"

"Seven as usual. It's beef in red wine."

"Is it OK if I go to Jenny's house round the corner? We are testing each other on our French for tomorrow?"

"Yes, that is a good idea, we don't want to have to worry about you going out walking on your own."

It was a gentle reminder that Dee had taken the plunge and gone out alone, and then ended up in a dangerous situation. Lydia had a lot of tact, and Dee knew she was right, it had been a foolhardy thing to do.

"I won't go out alone until they find out who tried to run me down!" she said with feeling. "And I will be back by seven."

"OK dear, I trust you. By the way, do you know why Jack is no longer cycling to school? Is there something wrong with his bike?"

Dee grinned. "He has just discovered girls, so he now likes to come on the bus with us."

Lydia looked startled. "Oh, is that all. Well he is sixteen."

Dee was glad she had not said anything yet, because if Jenny did turn out to be a suspicious character, then whether he liked it or not, Jack would have to be told about her, and he would have to listen. Right now he was so besotted, he thought the sun shone out of her.

She ran upstairs to her room, then changed out of her school uniform. It felt nice to put on some light shorts and a tee shirt. She could hear Jack's rap music pounding from his room, and soon Lydia would be asking him to turn it down, or use his headphones.

A glance at her watch showed it to be four thirty; another half hour before Jenny returned from her walk. She got her French revision out of her rucksack, and sat down trying to concentrate on it. But her mind was full of what she might discover at Jenny's house. It was going to be tricky with Jenny there, she could hardly search through cupboards and drawers in front of her, so there was no way to formulate a plan. She would just have to see if anything struck her as being unusual when she was at the house.

Her watch was now showing four forty-five, so she decided to walk round there anyway, and if Jenny's mother was not in, then she would wait outside. She gathered together her rucksack with all the books she needed inside, there was just a couple of weeks of exams left, then she could leave school for the summer.

She had planned to get a summer job to earn some extra pocket money. Even though her family was comfortably off, Dee and Jack had always been encouraged to earn their own pocket money and be independent. In Herne Bay, during the summer, there were always jobs going at local cafes and ice cream parlours.

Mario, at the ice cream parlour along the front, had offered her a part time job working three days a week. She had said she would check with her parents, but she was sure that they wouldn't mind. So once she had left school, that would be it for the summer, and she would still have time to herself as well.

She had arrived outside Jenny's house with just ten minutes to go now. Her mind returned to the task she had set herself. She didn't know what she might find out about Jenny in her house, but she had to try at the very least, because sometimes opportunities presented themselves when you least expected it.

She walked up to the front door and knocked, but there was no sign of a dog around, no barking or noise from within. Jenny might even come back late, after five o'clock, once she got walking the time would have slipped away. Suddenly there was a voice from within the house.

"Jenny, did you forget your key?"

Dee had never met Jenny's mother before, but the likeness was unmistakable as she stood there holding the side gate open. "Hello, are you looking for Jenny?"

162

"Yes, I am Dee, we were going to do some work together for our exam tomorrow."

"Oh yes, silly me, she did tell me. It's nice to meet you, Dee."

"I think I am a bit early, Mrs Latimer," Dee said very politely.

"No worries. Why don't you come in and get yourself a drink, she won't be long. I am just about to pop down to the town and get some food. When I opened the fridge, there wasn't much in it!"

She led Dee into the kitchen and filled up the kettle, then clicked it on. "Mugs are in the cupboard, help yourself, and I think there's a few biscuits left in the tin."

Dee smiled and thanked her, then watched her exit the back door and get into her car which was parked in the drive. Dee could not believe her luck. This made it much easier. If Jenny could stay out for a few more minutes, she could have a quick search round.

Ignoring the kettle, which had now clicked itself off, she looked quickly around the kitchen, which was very tidy, with just an electricity bill by the telephone on the worktop. She moved swiftly, opening drawers, but saw only menus from takeaway food shops, a couple of photos, nothing that could help her at all.

She rushed into the room behind, which was a through lounge. It had an old fashioned bureau at the other end, and it wasn't locked, so she pulled down the flap. Inside were both passports for Jenny and her mother, also one of a man with brown hair, the name inside said Julian Latimer. That was obviously Jenny's father, and the passport had expired last year.

Dee was beginning to realise how ridiculous all this was, as she didn't even know what she was looking for. Maybe a letter from 'the boss', proving they existed, and that there was a connection between them, but she knew how unlikely that would be. She remembered Beth's words; she had said Jenny had a crush on Billy. Well certainly there was nothing to indicate that, nor had Jenny seemed to realise that Jack was holding a torch for her. But was playing cool part of Jenny's plan to get in with her family, and was it Jenny who wanted rid of Dee? She shivered at the thought of it. The unknown was more frightening than she had imagined, not knowing who to trust, either. Nothing seemed to make any sense.

She opened the kitchen door and went out into the garden. There was a line full of washing, which was blowing gently in the breeze. It was quite a simply laid out garden, with a concrete patio at the top, then down a couple of steps to a lawn area, which had a path leading down the middle of the lawn where the washing line was. There were shrubs of various sizes and height on both sides. Set at the side, towards the end of the garden was a shed, which looked like it had seen better days, although it was still standing.

Dee wandered over to look through the window, and then she saw it, leaning against the wall on the far side was a motorbike. She reeled with shock, she had not been expecting this. But then she realised that her suspicions were right, and Jenny did have an ulterior motive for being her friend. To all intents and purposes, it looked like Jenny had tried to kill her!

Fear coursed through her. Jenny was a dangerous person and she needed to get out of here as fast as she could! Her dad needed to know, and the police, and of course, as painful as it might be, Jack had to be warned, too.

She picked up her rucksack and ran out of the side gate, not caring that she had left the back door unlocked. She couldn't bear to spend another minute here with Jenny pretending to be her friend. It was time for her to be exposed.

When she got home, Lydia was surprised to see her back so quickly. She was sitting in the conservatory with Nathan; both drinking a cup of tea. Nathan's face lit up. "Hello Dee, I thought Lydia said you were revising with Jenny."

Unable to contain herself any more, Dee burst out how she had gone round to Jenny's house to look for something suspicious. She explained that by chance she had looked in the shed, and there was a motorbike. It had frightened her so much, she had run home quickly. She finished off by saying that she would find it hard to tell Jack because he was so enamoured with Jenny, and could see no wrong in her.

"She is dangerous, Daddy. She tried to kill me. He must be warned, and we must also tell the police."

Nathan moved to comfort her, seeing her agitation. Dee was jumping to conclusions here, so he tried to be the voice of reason. "But maybe her dad rides the motorbike, he won't be the only person in the world to own one. You must admit it's a very unusual thing for a sixteen year old girl to do."

Dee became calmer. What her dad was saying made sense. Had she jumped to the wrong conclusion? It was not likely that Jenny's father would be trying to kill her. Seeing the motorbike had totally unnerved her, and her commonsense had deserted her.

It was at that moment, that Jack came into the room. He had heard Dee's agitated voice, and it was obvious something had upset her. He had no idea what it was, so curiosity had brought him down from his bedroom.

"Whatever is going on?"

Dee turned towards him, fully expecting her words to surprise him.

"Jack, did you know there is a motorbike in the shed at Jenny's house?"

Jack grinned. "Oh, that old thing. Apparently her dad used to ride it. He died three years ago, and it's been left to rust. I think it's falling apart, but she tried to suggest that I might like it. But when she showed it to me, I didn't like to say, but it's only fit to go down the tip."

Dee felt the wind go out of her sails. There was an embarrassed silence whilst Nathan and Lydia digested Jack's words.

"There you are, an innocent explanation," said Nathan awkwardly.

"You surely didn't link that bike to the rider on the bridge?" laughed Jack. "It doesn't even start."

Dee made no reply. It might sound amusing to Jack, but someone was definitely out to get her. Maybe it wasn't Jenny, but it was no wonder she felt like this. She was actually glad it wasn't Jenny, but it made her even more determined to find out who it was.

Just then her mobile rang, and it was a welcome diversion. It was Jenny, asking her where she had got to.

"So sorry," said Dee. "I came round, your mum saw me, but then I didn't feel well so I came home."

"Now Dee, don't worry about the exam, you'll be fine, that's all it is," said Jenny, and her voice sounded really kind. Dee felt guilty for the lie she had told, but she could hardly have told her the truth. This whole thing was getting out of hand now. "Thanks, Jenny. See you tomorrow," she said.

165

Chapter Twenty

As each day passed, Alan was enjoying being by the coast even more. The life was so different from London, where any journey by car involved queueing for miles behind cars and buses, taking an hour to travel two miles sometimes. He went by car to the train station, and parked it there all day, but here he had discovered the Thanet Way, which stretched all along the coast from Whitstable through to Broadstairs, so journeys were quick and enjoyable. Even travelling from Canterbury was bearable, as there were several different routes out of the city.

He had always believed that only retired people lived at the coast, but he had been told that the Kent coast did not close down during the winter. In Herne Bay several new housing estates had been built on green belt land, and a new doctor's practice had been set up to cope with the demand of more families in the area. In Beltinge a local superstore had been built, which not only stocked food, but also had an optician, holiday company, and an Argos, which delighted the local people, as they could shop there for virtually all their needs without needing to go down to the main town.

But all this modernisation had only improved the sleepy little seaside town of the past. It had not affected the beauty of the little village of Beltinge, nor the hamlet known as Bishopstone with the rugged cliffs and beaches, which remained the same, as did Reculver.

This part of the area held the most fascination for Alan. It was where the murder had taken place and all the suspects lived. He knew if he had a choice to live in the area, it was this part he would have chosen. It would have been just far enough from his in-laws to maintain a good family relationship. He knew they were not the sort of people to turn up on his doorstep every day, because they also had their own lives, but they would be there if either Zoe or himself needed them.

To be able to bring up Adam in this lovely clean area, away from all the crowds of London, and traffic pollution, would be amazing. But sadly this was only a dream. His job was at Wimbledon Police Station, and after her year of maternity leave was over, Zoe would return to work at Tooting hospital. In the meantime he was going to enjoy his time here. The team at Canterbury station were a great bunch, and Gary had proved to be very competent.

He had been as good as his word to Wendy, by allowing her to have the weekend off. Earlier that week had been a sad occasion. Janet's funeral had taken place. Her parents had decided to lay her to rest in this area, and then they were going back to London.

Sophie and Walter had asked if Alan and Wendy could attend, which did surprise him, but he felt it was the least they could do, especially as they had chosen to invite only close family. Knowing that Janet had not been popular at school had made them decide not to ask other members of her class to come along and remember her.

The one exception to that was Dee. Sophie had tried to put right the fact that Dee had been bullied by Janet, by inviting her. Dee really wasn't sure if she wanted to go. Her parents didn't interfere, as it was an important decision that only she could make. In the end she had come, and her nature being as it was, she told Sophie she had forgiven Janet. When he heard this, it seemed to prove to Alan that Dee had a kind and forgiving nature.

Billy had not been invited. He had not shown any grief at losing Janet, and this must have hurt her parents. So they had airbrushed him out of her life. When Alan stood next to Wendy at the side of the church, even he felt emotional when he saw Janet's picture. It had been put on a table near to the altar. Janet was smiling, and the wind was blowing her hair. To have her life extinguished so abruptly at sixteen yeas old was such a tragedy.

Sophie was sobbing quietly into a large white handkerchief, and a couple of rows further back he spotted Ava dabbing at her eyes with a tissue. The vicar had tried to keep a light note to the service by paying tribute to Janet's youth and enthusiasm for life, but there was a distinct air of sadness hanging over the gathering. Everyone knew she had been taken before her time in the most unimaginable circumstances, and it left a lingering sense of horror.

After it was over, Alan and Wendy very politely declined the invitation to go back to Sophie and Walter's house for refreshments. He was glad that Sophie and Walter had now been able to lay their daughter to rest, and it filled him with a new determination to try and find the killer quickly. There was a shadow hanging over this seaside town, and the funeral made it into all the local papers, and was discussed online and at news desks, even though they had done their best to keep it private, and not involve the local community.

Local reporters had not been allowed in the church, but there had been photos outside, where a local crowd had gathered. Curiosity had brought them there, and a local journalist had been getting a reaction from the crowd. They had said how tragic Janet's death had been, and then to add weight to his story, the journalist had finished off by saying that the murderer had yet to be found, which had struck a chord with Alan, and made him want to wrap it up soon.

Alan was glad when he got back to Whitstable after the funeral. He had seen many gruesome cases during his career, but none so far where the victim had been so young. Since he had become a father it seemed to affect him more. He guessed it must be the worst thing for a parent to bury their own child.

So when Ruth and Gerald told him about the production at the Marlowe, which was reputed to be both funny and entertaining, he jumped at the idea of taking Zoe. Now that they could text each other, and Ruth could send photos, Zoe felt more relaxed about leaving Adam, so they could both enjoy the evening without worrying.

They went to the theatre on Friday evening, and Alan had signed both himself and Wendy off for that weekend. But he did state that he would be on call if anything urgent came up. On Saturday he had put his shorts on, and they had walked with Adam right through

168

Whitstable and along the promenade to Tankerton, and then they sat in the gardens at the castle enjoying a cream tea.

Then, on Sunday, Gerald and Ruth decided to have a barbecue and invite a lot of their new friends. They were all impressed to meet Alan and know he was handling the case, but nobody asked him for any details, as they had all been told he would not be able to discuss it. He enjoyed socialising with them, and he felt very proud of Adam, as everyone was admiring his son. It was such a change for him to be relaxing with a couple of beers. It was a weekend he would remember, because his phone had not rung with an emergency situation which would mean he had to go in to work. This was so unusual. Although Zoe was used to it by now, and she never had complained, it was easier whilst they were staying with her parents. By the time the weekend ended, he was even more motivated to solve this case; the rest had really done him good.

Billy was beginning to relax a bit more now. It had been a couple of weeks since his interview with the cops, he hadn't been arrested, and they had not come back. Having his father around for a week had made him feel much safer. He knew Ricky would arrange a lawyer for him if necessary, but it hadn't come to that yet.

It gave him a feeling of self importance that his father was an FBI man. But it was also ironic, when Billy thought about his past. This had been excused as 'growing up'. Having Ricky around was calming, and his dad made sure that during that week they spent time together.

They had gone to Canterbury and seen the Cathedral, more for Ricky's benefit, as he took a lot of photos, and they had enjoyed a few pub lunches. Ricky knew it was a typically English thing to do, and he loved an English pub, as his home country only had bars which had no history or character whatsoever.

Billy had enjoyed the time spent with him, but by the end of that week he was happy to know that Ricky was flying back. Obviously it meant that he was unlikely to be arrested, and also he was getting his freedom back; he could do what he wanted.

After Ricky had departed, Billy had visited Nathan and Lydia

h

again with his grandparents. He was curious to know what had been going on, so he didn't mind going. Philip and Isabel were absolutely determined to keep the family ties going, so whilst he was in England, they made regular visits. He heard that someone had sent Dee a note accusing her of killing Janet, and then shortly after that she had been almost run down by someone on a motorbike on the bridge at Bishopstone. Naturally all the family, as well as Dee, were really upset about that, and the police were taking it seriously, as Dee now had police protection when she went out. He found it all very intriguing, especially as there was no way that Dee would have killed Janet. She was far too shy and quiet, and she just didn't have it in her. But it did sound as though someone was out to get Dee, and make her accountable for Janet's death.

The next thing he found out was that Janet had been taunting Dee about their mother, and he then realised he had known very little about Janet. He had never bothered to find out anything about her, as their meetings had been mainly for sex. It seemed she had been lonely, without many friends, and even though he would never admit it to anyone, he had experienced guilt since she died. He had not treated her well. He knew how much better he would feel if only the police could find someone and charge them for her murder.

All of this had been learned through his family, because the local journalists didn't really know much at all. It felt to him like a Hollywood movie, and who would have thought it would all be going on in this sleepy seaside town.

It looked like he would be staying around for a while, and it suited him fine. Sunshine, walks on the beach, doting grandparents, and a possible place at college in September. He had it made here!

Something deep inside drove him to take that walk again. He set off from his grandparents' house. It was very windy today, and there was something very majestic about the waves crashing against the rocks and the cries of the seagulls. The tide was halfway out, the wet sand exposed, with rock pools all along the beach, and right at the back of the beach was the shingle which led up to the rugged cliffs with the shallow caves where both Dee and Janet had been found. Caves or cubby holes, but just big enough for a body to lay inside.

His mind went back to the panic he had felt when Dee had fainted right in front of him, and his desperate attempt to drag her up the beach so she couldn't drown when the tide turned. Then the realisation that she needed help. He could still remember how he had run as fast as he could to that phone box, completely forgetting that the police would trace his fingerprints, but panic had set in, and he couldn't think straight.

For all of his life he had always been quick to take offence, and he had an uncontrollable temper. When that red mist descended, he became very angry, and then afterwards he just couldn't remember what had happened. This was what had happened with Terry Harris, seeing him trying to make out with Barbara, who Billy believed belonged to him, had enraged him, and afterwards they had told him he had broken Terry's nose, but Billy had no memory of that.

Then it had happened again with Janet. When she had announced that she was six weeks pregnant, all his hopes of going to college in England were ruined. He was sure his family would insist that he had to marry her, or at the very least support Janet and the baby. He had felt that red mist swirling around him. He had tried so hard to remember what happened after that, but he couldn't. His only memory of that afternoon was seeing Dee, and dragging her up to what he considered safety.

He couldn't help feeling such fear when he thought about Janet. Maybe his mind had blocked it out because it was so horrendous, he just didn't know. Had he, in fact, killed her? And, more importantly, had he got away with it?

Jenny couldn't help wondering if the police were likely to make an arrest soon. She was pleased with herself that her acting skills were so good, but of course she was courting danger by lying to the police. Even as close as she was to her mother, she had not shared the fact that she had lied to them. The day that Janet died, she had not walked along to Tankerton, it had been towards Reculver, and although it had been much earlier than all the happenings that day on the beach, which was why she hadn't seen them, she had been in the vicinity. The only person she had met was Janet, who had clearly been on her way to meet Billy, and she had only missed seeing Dee and Beth because they must have been at the bus stop when she passed by.

She had also lied about 'the boss'. She was just as scared as all the others of this unknown person who had posted vile stuff to Dee on Facebook. Jenny had felt sorry for Janet when she first joined St Martha's, she was clearly a loner. Jenny had been there since she was eleven, but Janet arrived at the age of fourteen, and in the beginning they had struck up a friendship. She couldn't help noticing that Janet was shy and lacking confidence.

At that time, Dee had been a popular member of the class. Then Beth arrived, and immediately struck up a close friendship with Dee. Beth had a way with her that appealed to everyone, and she had never heard a bad word said against her.

But it wasn't long before everything changed. Janet became spiteful towards Dee, and then Dee lost all her friends except Beth, who had stayed firm in her support. Jenny challenged Janet about it, and that is when she found out about 'the boss'.

Janet seemed to be in great fear of this person who fed her so many details about Dee's mother Sadie. Janet even said she had been threatened with death. Regretfully Jenny had ended her friendship with Dee, it was just all too complicated to get involved with her any more. But it seemed the worm had turned when Janet told Jenny she had had enough, she no longer wanted to taunt Dee, because she liked her and felt she was a good person. She said she didn't care what her mother had done, it was history now. Such brave words, but then Janet had lost her life.

When Jenny had first heard about Janet's death, her first thought was had Janet been pushed too far, and taken her own life. But when it became a murder inquiry, fear of the unknown had swept over her, as she had no doubt that Janet had been murdered because she had defied 'the boss'.

Jenny had been too scared to open up and tell the police because, who knows, she might be the next victim. But she had tried to make it right with Dee. It was noticeable that after Janet died, Dee had been accepted back as a friend by the others in her class. Jenny couldn't criticise them for being like sheep, she had been just as guilty, but she felt more comfortable since she had made it right. However, the shadow of evil, created by 'the boss', hung like a heavy impenetrable curtain over them all.

Chapter Twenty-one

"Mum, for goodness sake, you can't lay in bed all day!"

"I haven't got long to live, you know."

Beth knew she was wasting her words, her mother hadn't even got a clue what day it was. She was a most unpredictable woman, laying in bed professing to be dying one minute, then out all night roaming the fields and the beaches, causing mayhem wherever she went.

But she was the only mother that Beth had ever known, and she loved and hated her in equal measure. The strain of keeping her mother a secret from the very exclusive private school she attended had been hard. But, over the years, Beth had learned to cover up the truth and deceive people; she had to survive herself in life and it had been the only way.

Nature had bestowed on Beth an innocent and very pretty face, with wide doll-like blue eyes, golden hair, which she was careful to wear in plaits to keep her naïve image intact, and a charisma that drew people to her naturally.

Beth had vowed she would never make the mistakes that Lizzie had. Her mother had been a promising student with an ambition to become a barrister. She was multi-talented and beautiful. Her blonde looks, slim frame, and alluring green eyes, meant that once they met her, nobody could forget Lizzie.

So after getting very high grades in her A-levels, Lizzie had decided to take a year out and travel before she took up the place she had been offered at Oxford University. She had always had an ambition to travel the world, and she felt that this was now a golden opportunity. Her parents had other ideas. They were not rich, but they both had jobs and their own home in London. Neither of them had been as bright as Lizzie and they were very proud of her, and wanted her to reach her full potential.

Their idea had been for her to go straight to university, do her courses and then graduate. Her dad was going to take out a loan to support her whilst she was at university, with the idea that once she got a well paid job, she could help him to pay it back. But Lizzie had her mind fixed on going round the world, so nothing was going to stop her. She duly set off, leaving her very disgruntled parents at home.

During her travels she met a man, and became pregnant. From then onwards her life fell apart. She was totally obsessed with her baby's father, so no way would she contemplate an abortion, which is what Beth would have done. This baby was a link with her lover, and she would never leave him. According to Lizzie, although he was married, he had promised he would leave his wife and children and they could then have a life together.

So Lizzie hung around. He was giving her money secretly and, when Beth was born, Lizzie said he had absolutely adored his new daughter. They even formulated a plan to escape together, and then suddenly he had died, so it had never happened. Lizzie was so grief-stricken that she gradually started to lose her mind.

Beth had no way of knowing if her mother spoke the truth, as Lizzie lived in a fantasy world most of the time. So Beth grew up with only a mother, and when she started school, it was clear that she had inherited her mother's above average intelligence. She shone at school and made friends easily, and at quite a young age, she made up her mind she would not end up like her mother, living on benefits. She would put her brains to good use.

After they returned to England, they were living in Brighton in a very modest one bedroom studio, which Beth hated. Her mother had the bedroom, and Beth slept on the sofa in the lounge.

Sometimes Beth felt if only she could leave her mother, she might have a chance to have a normal life. Lizzie had become paranoid about a lot of things. She had started to take drugs, and most of the time she lived in a fantasy world. Her moods veered between deep depression, and extreme happiness and ecstasy. Beth assumed she was controlled by the drugs she was taking. But how could she leave the one person she was related to in the whole world? She had never met her grandparents, or even knew where they lived, as once Lizzie had gone her own way and become pregnant, they had airbrushed her from their life.

But one thing Lizzie still had was her looks. And one day, when they were sunbathing on the beach at Brighton, Ian Wood had come into their lives. He was very taken with Lizzie, and her golden haired and sweet natured little daughter. It was the first time for ages that anyone had taken any notice of Lizzie, because she spent most of her time at home in bed, saying that she was dying. But on this particularly warm sunny day, Beth had managed to get her to come to the beach.

For a while Lizzie became almost normal in her behaviour after she met Ian. He was a handsome man in his early thirties with brown hair and hazel eyes. He stood about six feet tall, and when the holiday ended, it was clear that he was totally captivated by Lizzie.

He asked Lizzie and Beth to come home to Herne Bay and live with him. He felt to Beth like a gallant knight on a white charger who had come to rescue Lizzie from herself. Beth's hopes had been that when they moved in with Ian, her mother might realise what a good man she had, and stop fantasising about someone who was now dead and no longer a part of her life.

But coming to Herne Bay was the worst thing they could have done. It was where Sadie had lived, the woman Lizzie hated most of all, and to make matters worse, she lived on in her daughter Dee, who was in Beth's class at school.

When Beth met Dee she had bonded with her straightaway, she had felt a connection. But it was the same love/hate relationship that she had with her mother. If only Dee had left the school and moved away, then maybe her mother might not have driven herself mad, and become impossible for poor unsuspecting Ian to live with. In the end it was inevitable that they would split up, and Beth's chance of a normal life had now gone.

Ian had been so good to Beth. Not only had he paid for her school fees when they were all together, he continued to pay for them after he had split up with Lizzie. He recognised how intelligent Beth was, and just because her mother had ruined her own life, he didn't think it fair that Beth should suffer for that. He had told her she could stay with him when her mother moved out, as she wasn't the problem, but some sort of instinctive loyalty, which even she didn't understand, had kept her with Lizzie .

There was a certain prestige about being a pupil at St Martha's, so Beth knew she had to carry on the charade that she still lived at Riverside Walk. It was a nice house with four bedrooms, built in old fashioned cottage style on an estate with others, in a perfect situation, with trees and a stream running by. Her bedroom had been very spacious, and Ian had bought her every bit of modern technology that there was, but that was all in the past now.

After they left, Lizzie had been unable to hold down a job for any length of time. So they now had to live on benefits. The old, damp and very smelly cottage where they now lived was so bad, it should really have been condemned. It was a semi-detached two up and two down, and the other half was unoccupied because of how bad it was.

It was this life that she had now been subjected to that caused Beth to envy Dee so much. But there was a part of Beth that really cared for Dee as well. She felt so mixed up about her feelings for her. In her mind, it was Sadie that had caused her mother's downfall, and if she hadn't, then maybe Beth and her mother would not be living in such poverty. And maybe her mother wouldn't be acting so weirdly.

To see Dee living in a house which was so grand, and being brought up in such a wealthy situation, with parents who loved and cared about her, even if they were not blood relatives, really stuck in her throat.

And as each day passed, her mother seemed to be getting worse. She would lay in bed and pretend to be ill, then wait until Beth went out and go and do something outrageous. Beth never knew what she was going to come home to, but at the same time, she couldn't bear to stay around the place, it was so depressing. Lizzie had now even taken to dressing in all black and whirling round at high speed on the motorbike that she had ever since she was a teenager, and had been previously stored in the garage at Ian's house up until the time they left.

Admittedly Lizzie was only thirty-five, as she had become a mother at nineteen, but riding around on a motorbike, and scaring the hell out of people like Dee, was not a sane thing to do. When she realised just what her mother had done, Beth was filled with horror, and so relieved that the police didn't know their true address, and that they did not have neighbours nearby.

She knew from past experience, that it was a waste of time trying to get her mother out of bed, and she wasn't going to stay around today. The spell of warm sunny weather had temporarily ended, and a north wind was blowing. The sky was grey and overcast.

In the shed, next to the motorbike, was a bicycle that she hadn't used for ages. She wasn't even sure it was rideable, but she got it out and tried to blow some of the dust off it. Then she spotted that the tyres were flat and, although she hunted round, she couldn't find a foot pump or a puncture repair outfit. It was probably at Ian's house, as he had always maintained her bike in the past. So she abandoned her idea of riding it, and put it back.

Even though the weather was not great, she felt she needed to get out today. They had been doing exams all week and, because of her unstable lifestyle with Lizzie, Beth had perfected the art of not allowing anything else to interrupt her learning, so she felt fairly confident that she had done well. It was now her time to relax, and that was only really possible when she was away from her mother.

Lately when Dee went out, she seemed to have a police escort; ever since stupid Lizzie had nearly run her down on her motorbike. They didn't walk with Dee, but kept a watchful eye on her, so Beth felt she couldn't really keep company with her, as she needed to keep the police out of her life at all times. In trying to keep her erratic mother a secret, there were times when she felt like she was walking a very tight line, and it would be so easy to fall off the rope.

She felt a bit jealous of Jenny, ever since she had become friendly with Dee again. She was happy when Dee mistrusted Jenny, and Dee thought she was out to get her, but after realising she was wrong about Jenny, Dee had forged an even stronger bond with her. They now spent time together, much to Beth's annoyance. She had realised that it was inevitable, as they only lived a road apart from one another. Dee confided her inmost secrets to Beth, so she now knew about Dee's visit to Jenny's house, and the discovery of her late father's old motorbike. Jenny had never mentioned the death of her father, surprisingly, so neither of them had realised. Beth had wished a thousand times that her mother hadn't gone out and scared Dee on that motorbike. As it stood there in the shed, or sometimes even against the wall of the house, it would be such a giveaway if the police ever came round.

Athough she wasn't sure who she could now spend time with, she decided to walk into Herne Bay. She could always wander round the shops, then go to the bandstand and get a coffee. She put on her hooded waterproof coat just in case the grey skies heralded rain, that way she wouldn't get caught out.

Every time she walked along the front now, and glimpsed the cave, she kept thinking about Janet, she couldn't help it. Why had Janet rebelled? If only she hadn't, she would still be alive. What had started as simply a mission to rid themselves of Dee to another school, or, better still, getting her to move right away from the Herne Bay area, had become so much worse. It had ended up as murder.

Dee was so glad it was the weekend. She had tried very hard with her exam papers, and was hoping when they got the results in the summer holidays, that she would have passed at least some of them. She had felt really bad about misjudging Jenny, and thinking that she wanted to harm her, and then getting the wrong end of the stick when she saw the motorbike. She hadn't even realised that Jenny's father had died, but then they hadn't been close friends again until recently. Thank goodness Jack had known about the motorbike, because she knew that her dad would have been ready to go straight round to the police station and report it.

Anyway, their friendship was good now again, and she had been for a couple of walks with Jenny and Rex after heeding her parents warnings about walking on her own. There was also the comfort of knowing that the police were keeping an eye on her. They kept at a discreet distance when she was out, but it would be enough to deter anyone who had any ideas.

She glanced out of the window, and could see a man in plain clothes hovering at the corner of the street. It wasn't a particularly nice day, the sky was grey, so she didn't really fancy going for a walk. Maybe Beth would like to go to the cinema this afternoon. They had not been since the day that Janet died, or they could go for a swim at the baths.

Dee picked up her phone and sent Beth a text. When Beth saw it, she really was missing Dee, so she thought to hell with the escort, they were nowhere near to where she lived! She replied to say she was already on her way into Herne Bay on the bus, so they could meet up. Dee then suggested she could meet her at the bus stop. Well, of course, Beth didn't want that, as she was not coming from Greenhill, so she sent a reply saying she had already got off the bus, and would see Dee inside Makcari's at the bandstand, where they could have a coffee and catch up.

Dee agreed to that and, pulling on her jacket, she called out to Lydia that she was going into town for a bit to have a coffee and meet Beth.

"Dad's going into town. He wants to get himself a few bits at Boots before we go on holiday," called out Lydia.

Dee hesitated, it wasn't that nice a day to walk, so a lift from her dad would be handy.

"OK, thanks. I will wait then," she said, and then went into the kitchen where her parents were.

"Where's Jack?" she asked idly.

"Lazy tyke; he's not up yet," laughed Lydia.

"Well it's been a week of exams," Dee reminded her.

"I know. Not much longer, and then you have time to yourself."

"Oh, that reminds me, Mario has offered me a holiday job; three days a week at the ice cream parlour," explained Dee.

"Sounds good to me. You can stand on your own two feet, and buy your own clothes and shoes," said Nathan, laughing. It was a standing joke about how much Dee liked having new things. Dee smiled back. She knew her dad would approve.

180

"Maybe we should get Jack out on a paper round instead of laying in bed," said Lydia, also laughing.

As they left the house in Nathan's car, the policeman saw them.

"Good to see they are keeping watch," remarked Nathan. "Where would you like me to drop you?"

"Outside the bandstand would be great. I am meeting Beth for a coffee and then a look around the shops. If we decide to go to the cinema I will text Lydia and let her know."

"OK, don't spend all that money before you have earned it," laughed Nathan, as she kissed him on the cheek and got out of the car.

When Dee got inside Makcari's, Beth had not yet arrived. She noticed that it had been redecorated since she last came in. The inside had been painted a very pretty shade of green, which made it appear very restful. She sat down at a table in the corner whilst she waited for Beth to arrive.

After a few minutes she saw Beth. They had not seen much of each other at school, as they had been in different rooms to take their exams. Dee had always been a naturally demonstrative person since a small child, so she found herself hugging Beth because she had missed her, and Beth hugged her back.

"Take off your coat, and I will order us both a coffee," Dee said hospitably.

Beth smiled her thanks and sat down. "No police escort then?" she said softly, as Dee returned to the table with the coffees.

"Not today. Daddy gave me a lift down."

That news made Beth feel a lot more comfortable. So they drank their coffee and compared notes, trying to second guess how well they might have fared in their exams. After about half an hour, it looked as though the sky was getting lighter. The clouds were moving and the sun was trying to peep through.

"Maybe it won't rain after all," remarked Dee.

"Let's go for a wander round the shops now," suggested Beth. And they linked arms and walked out of Makcari's, crossed the road, and made their way towards the high street.

Chapter Twenty-two

Lizzie waited until Beth had gone. She knew Beth was going out with that Morton Brown girl again and she didn't like that at all. That family had ruined her life, and she was determined that somehow Dee would pay.

She got herself out of bed and dressed in her black riding gear. It made her feel so powerful, and invincible. She hated this rathole they now had to live in. She should have been living the high life right now with her only true love, but that cursed family had deprived her of that.

It wasn't the best day for a ride out, but she didn't care. She fancied riding past Reculver Towers, and then going fast along the Saxon Walk as far as Minnis Bay. She didn't care if she met the occasional dog walker; she flashed past them so quickly they didn't have time to say anything to her.

Lizzie knew that Beth hated her using her motorbike, and if Beth could get rid of it, she would. So she laughed at the sheer exhilaration of doing what she wanted to, and absolutely pleasing herself, and not giving a damn about anyone else.

Today being quite grey and murky, just as she had thought, she didn't see many dog walkers. She had the promenade to herself, so she got up to a high speed and was enjoying the wind on her face.

By the time she arrived back at the house, it was lunchtime. She left her motorbike standing outside, leaning against the decaying wall of the shed, and went to get a drink. She wasn't that hungry, but it was time to take her medication, so she did herself one slice of toast to help it down.

Her mobile beeped, and when she checked it Beth had sent her a message:

HOPE YOU ARE UP. I AM OFF TO THE
CINEMA WITH DEE. SEE YOU LATER.

That name inflamed her so much. How could Beth spend time with her when she knew what that family had done to them? She knew she would have to put a stop to it once and for all. Her last mission on the bridge had failed because her interfering stepbrother had come along, but this time Lizzie would make sure she got it right. She vowed to herself that later today she would strike, and this time she would make sure that Dee paid for her mother's deeds. There would be retribution.

Dee and Beth came out of the cinema; it was six o'clock. Nathan had said he would pick her up after the film if she sent him a text, and he would also run Beth home. Beth had at first refused, but Nathan had insisted, so she realised she would have to get a bus back from Greenhill once his car had gone. Deceptions like this made her life far more complicated.

Nathan was very cheerful when he arrived. It had done Dee good to go out with Beth after a week of exams, and he felt pleased to see her so happy and upbeat. He drove over to Greenhill to drop Beth off and, when they reached Riverside Walk, she insisted that he stop at the beginning of the road and she could walk down to her house. He turned the car round to go back, and Beth was waving to them, and then she was gone.

When they got home the policeman had gone for the day. Nathan had told him earlier that he was going down to the town to pick Dee up, so he could finish for that day. Dee was glad he had gone, as she felt embarrassed to have a police escort, and was hoping they would soon catch the killer so her life could go back to normal.

Nathan had jumped into the shower before his dinner was ready, and Lydia had suddenly realised she had run out of gravy granules.

183

She didn't want her roast chicken to spoil, so she asked Dee to keep an eye on it whilst she popped to the local shop, which was just a couple of minutes away.

"Don't worry, I can pop up there and get them for you," said Dee. "It won't take me long."

"Are you sure? I would normally ask Jack to go on his bike, but he isn't in yet."

"It's fine," said Dee. She ran out of the house. The smell of the roast chicken was most inviting, and she knew dad would be smothering his dinner in gravy, that was how he liked it. She headed towards the shops just at the end of Seaview Road.

The fact that it was broad daylight did not deter Lizzie. She sprang out of an alleyway, totally taking Dee by surprise. She knocked her to the ground, just as if she was an irritating fly. Then she picked up her prostrate body and bundled her into the boot of her old jalopy, which had seen much better days.

Lizzie didn't bother to check whether anyone had seen her. The car groaned protestingly, and then shuddered into action. She drove towards Reculver, exulting to herself that she had finally got Dee. She had been drinking all afternoon, and if anyone had stopped her, she would have been booked immediately. But she didn't know what fear was. She was on a high; she was so drunk she was weaving all over the road.

She had planned the capture of Dee very carefully, and it had nearly misfired. When she saw Nathan driving past with Dee in the car, and then driving through the gates which closed behind him, and up the drive, she had been very angry, swearing and cursing because it had all gone wrong.

She was about to give up and drive home, when suddenly she saw Dee run out of the front of the house and through a little gate. This was further up the road from where she was parked, so she positioned herself in the alley where her car was parked, all ready to surprise her when she passed, and it had worked!

It was no good taking Dee back to the house, as Beth would mess it up for her, she knew it. She was planning to kill her, but she wanted her to suffer emotionally first, just like Lizzie had all these years. She wanted to make her squirm before she died, to suffer physically because of how she and her mother had made Lizzie suffer mentally. The time had now come for her to pay!

When she reached Reculver she drove her spluttering car down an unmade road, which led to a field. In that field was a deserted old caravan which would soon be used to house fruit pickers for the summer season, but by the time that they used it, she would have killed this creature! She could hear muffled sounds coming from the boot, and she laughed mockingly. The bitch was coming round, so she stopped outside the caravan, angrily flinging the boot open, and before Dee could say anything she hit her full in the face, causing her mouth to bleed.

"Shut up, you bitch. I have a lot I want to say to you!"

Alan was about to sit down for his dinner when the call came through. Nathan had reported Dee missing. She had popped out to go to a local shop, and had not returned. The duty constable said he had been really upset and feared her life was in danger.

Alan's mouth had been watering at the sight of the pork chop he was about to eat, but now he had to turn his back on it, and go to work. More importantly, he could not share bath time with Adam tonight. Duty called, and this might well be a dangerous situation.

"Honey, I am so sorry, I have been called in," he said apologetically.

"It's OK, you go," said Zoe. She knew if it was out of hours, then it would be important.

Alan rang Wendy and explained the situation quickly. She said she would be ready and standing by the door when he arrived. She would also miss dinner, but it seemed like Dee might be in danger, so they couldn't afford to waste any time. When she got in the car, Alan did his best to further explain the situation.

"Apparently Dee had been out with Beth during the day. Her dad picked her up from the cinema about six, and took them both home, dropping off Beth at Riverside Walk. At home her dad got in the shower, and Dee popped round the shop, which is just two minutes away. The duty policeman had gone home."

"And she didn't come back?" asked Wendy, wonderingly.

"That's right, and Nathan believes her life is in danger, and I am inclined to agree with him."

Wendy felt very alarmed. "We tried to protect her, but it didn't work."

"Yes, we failed her!"

Alan didn't dwell on that, there was no point because time was of the essence now.

"Can you rustle up a couple of volunteer officers to knock on a few doors on the way to the shops, to see if anyone saw anything. Then ring Beth's mobile. She saw her last."

Wendy busied herself on her mobile, while Alan drove the car. She managed to get the volunteers, but for some reason she could not connect with Beth, the mobile just rang out.

"I can't get Beth, she is not picking up."

"OK, that decides it for me. We are going to Riverside Walk."

By the time they reached Greenhill it was past eight o'clock, but still light. When they knocked at the door, they could hear sounds of the TV on, and then a man answered the door. Remembering they were in plain clothes, Alan got out his identification to show the man.

"Good evening, I am DCI Alan Clarke, and this is WPC Wendy Stuart. Is Beth in?"

Ian Wood was completely taken by surprise. He assumed that after Beth and Lizzie had moved out, they would have given their new address. He couldn't help wondering why the police wanted Beth. It was Lizzie who behaved outrageously, not her daughter. He had always felt sorry for Beth. She had not had an easy life with her unstable mother, and he had always told her there was a home with him if she wanted it.

"I think you best come in."

They entered the hall, and Alan explained. "Dee Edwards is a close friend of Beth's, and they were out together today. But Dee has now gone missing, and we wondered if Beth had any idea as to where Dee might be now."

"I can't answer that. Maybe they have met up again, but Lizzie and Beth moved out of here over a year ago now, and they live at Reculver."

186

"Really!" Alan's brain was whirling. That meant Beth's alibi was false, and she had taken a lot of trouble to let Dee think she still lived here when she saw her onto the bus. Of course, she could come here regularly maybe. After all, they had seen her here a couple of weeks ago. He decided to check it out with Ian.

"Does Beth visit you much?"

"Not as much as I would like. Beth is a sweet girl, but I am afraid Lizzie has issues."

"I see. Well our main concern right now is finding Dee. Can you give me their new address?"

Ian went to get it. He had never visited the house because he had a memory of a couple of tumbledown semi-detached cottages, and he knew it was not a good environment for Beth to be growing up in. He had been given the address so their mail could be forwarded when they first went there.

"Thanks very much for your time," said Wendy, and they left the house and got back into the car.

"She wanted us to think she lived there that day we called round, so her alibi is not safe!" declared Alan, as he was driving towards Reculver. "I don't care how sweet and lovely he thinks she is. Remember, Wendy, it's often the person you least expect."

When they arrived at the cottage, Alan hesitated. Surely nobody lived here, it looked as if it might have been condemned. The whole cottage was barely standing; the window frames were broken and hanging down. But inside them a light could be seen, as although it wasn't dusk yet, obviously the interior was very dark. Whoever was inside needed the light on.

He wasted no time on preliminaries, rapping on the bare wood, which splintered into his hands. "Open up. It's the police here, and it's urgent!"

There were signs of movement inside, then slowly the door creaked open. Beth stood there, her face was pale and her innocent blue eyes looked worried. What a damn good actress she was, thought Alan.

"I am so glad you are both here. It's my mother; she isn't well, and she does unpredictable things. She's gone out in her old car, which is practically falling apart, and it isn't safe. I am worried about her."

Alan didn't wait for an invitation, he stepped into the dank hall, and Wendy followed. It smelled as though it had wood rot. There was a window at the side with a broken pane. It was filthy, and difficult to see through, but he spotted a shed, and there leaning against it was a motorbike. So Dee hadn't imagined it; they were definitely at the right place!

"So where is Dee, then? You spent all day with her. And why didn't you answer your phone?"

"My phone is in the kitchen, charging, but never mind that. How can Dee be missing? Her dad took her home and he dropped me off too!"

Alan walked through to the dingy room which had the light on. Spotting a mobile phone on the table, he went to pick it up."

"No, not that one, and it's private!" said Beth, instinctively trying to stop him.

Alan adopted a stern manner. Her vulnerability was not lost on him, but he thought it was an act. He handed the phone to Wendy.

"Nothing is private when we are investigating a murder inquiry."

Beth went even paler. "I didn't kill Janet, honestly."

Her heart was sinking as Wendy glanced through the texts. She had always been so careful to keep this phone separate. Everything was coming out now, but more importantly a sixth sense told her that her mother must have Dee. How she had managed with police around was a mystery, but her mother was capable of anything. She wished she had done something about Lizzie before, because, if she had completely lost her mind, Dee would be in grave danger.

"A lot of the replies to your texts refer to you as 'the boss'," said Wendy.

"I can explain that."

"You certainly can, down at the station," said Alan, smoothly. "We have a lot of evidence here, you know. The phone, and the motorbike, you can explain it all at the station. I am giving you one last chance to tell the truth: Where is Dee?"

"I really don't know where she is; please believe me."

Alan didn't want to put handcuffs on her. He honestly didn't want to believe that Dee's closest friend had tried to kill her, but there was so much evidence against her right now. As for this hellhole she lived in, they needed to get health and safety round here. No one should be living in a place like this. His tone softened: "We are taking you in for further questioning, you can explain everything to us at the station."

Lizzie was feeling very pleased with herself; she had done really well today. She had captured the bitch and she was now safely tied up inside a caravan. She planned to go home and go to bed now. If Beth was in, she would deny all knowledge of kidnapping the bitch. Tomorrow she intended to return to the caravan to let her know just how much she had ruined Lizzie's life; her and her mother too. Then she would set fire to the caravan with her inside, and all of her fancy life and the money she had would mean nothing, because she wouldn't be around to enjoy it.

It made her laugh to think she would go up in smoke, and she would be in fear all of tonight, not knowing what was going to happen to her. And it was just what she deserved!

As she drove towards her cottage, she saw the police car outside. She wasn't surprised, police had a habit of catching up with you. But she was invincible, and she would always be one step ahead. She still had her black outfit on, so she couldn't let them see her.

She always felt great when she wore her black leathers, like a devil woman; it was fun! She parked off the road. Once they realised that Dee wasn't there, then they would go.

When she saw them come out and get in the police car, she noticed that Beth was with them. That was perfect for Lizzie. Whilst they were questioning Beth, they wouldn't be searching for Dee. In her drunken state, she had convinced herself that once she set the caravan alight, there would be no trace of Dee.

She drove the car round to the back of the cottage. It was getting dark now. She got out and stumbled towards the front door, and pushed at it. It creaked open and she made her way through the darkness and into her bedroom. Then she took off her black leather outfit and stroked it lovingly.

On her bed was her nightwear, which she put on. Then she switched the light on. Inside the kitchen was another light, and she opened up the cupboard, found a tin of soup, then heated it up in an ancient and rusty microwave. There wasn't any bread, so she just had the soup.

After drinking all day long, she could feel weariness attacking her, so she decided to go to bed. She could pretend to be asleep when Beth came in, and avoid any sort of questioning. Without a second thought about what might be happening to her daughter, Lizzie closed her eyes and was soon asleep.

Chapter Twenty-three

Alan arranged for police officers with sniffer dogs to comb the surrounding countryside to search for Dee. The local press, radio, and news stations had all been alerted. He honestly didn't know if they would find her alive or dead, but what he did know was, this blue-eyed and innocent girl, who professed to be Dee's best friend, was in it right up to her neck.

He faced Beth across the table, and Wendy sat recording the interview. First he read her her rights.

"Interview with Beth Harper commenced at twenty-one hundred hours. Miss Harper does not have a solicitor at this time."

Beth was sobbing, but he refused to be moved by her. Wendy silently handed her a box of tissues. Alan scanned the notes that Wendy had made, very quickly.

"Beth, tears are not going to get you out of this. You say you are Dee's best friend, yet there is evidence on that mobile that you are 'the boss', the person who controlled all the class as well as Janet in an effort to destroy Dee."

Beth gulped and he continued. "We found a motorbike at your house, just like the one Dee described as being driven straight at her, and you don't live at the address you gave to us, which makes your alibi for the day that Janet died unsafe."

She could feel her hands shaking, and Beth had never been more scared in her life. They hadn't listened when she told them about her mother, they thought she was lying. She made a supreme effort to pull herself together. She would make them listen, and she prayed with all her heart that Dee could be found before her mother struck again.

She spoke in a faltering voice, "I have done some bad things, I know, but I do genuinely care for Dee, and I don't know where she is, and I am scared for her. So please listen to me."

Something about her demeanour made Alan think that she was sincere. His methods of finding out the truth were always to listen first, so he nodded. "Go on then, explain."

Beth cleared her throat. "My mother took a year off after she passed her A-levels, and went on a world trip. Whilst she was in Spain, she had an affair with Danny Foster, the famous footballer, and became pregnant with me. . ."

Alan and Wendy exchanged glances, knowing exactly what this meant. . . "So you are Dee's half-sister."

"I was born six months before Dee, although we are in the same year at school. My mother has always insisted that Danny was going to leave his wife and marry her, and to this day she is still obsessed with him, so much that she seems to have lost all reason."

"But what has that got to do with Dee?"

"My mother is convinced that Sadie murdered Danny, even though it was an open verdict. She is also very jealous of the fact that he had an affair with Sadie and Dee was the result, so she blames Sadie and Dee for robbing her of a happy life."

Alan could not help his next words. "Does it ever occur to your mother that Danny Foster was a scumbag, who got two women pregnant whilst being married to someone else? Does she honestly believe she could have had any sort of happiness with him?"

"She doesn't look at it that way. He was the love of her life."

Alan guessed that, although Beth knew what he meant, her mother needed to blame someone else for her own failings, but now it had got really serious, and led to murder.

"We all make our own happiness in life," he said pointedly, "but what concerns me is you came to this school hell-bent on ruining Dee's life."

Beth bowed her head. "I did, and for that I deserve to be punished. If we hadn't moved to Herne Bay, my mother might have kept her sanity."

Alan looked puzzled, he still couldn't quite grasp it. So Beth continued.

"We came to England when I was a baby, and we lived at Brighton. My mother met Ian Wood, and for a while she became almost normal. Ian is a good man. She stopped raving on about losing the love of her life, and then Ian asked us to come and live with him at Herne Bay. Neither of us knew that Dee lived there. Ian had plans to marry my mother, and for the first time in my life, I felt we might be a normal family.

"So what happened then?"

"When my mother found out the Morton Browns were here, and that Dee was in my class, she became obsessed again, and desperate to get her own revenge. It ruined her relationship with Ian, so we had to move out. All my life I have been told that this family are bad news, so to protect my mother I had to try and coerce Dee into leaving the school and the district. But although I had hated the very mention of her name, I found myself getting really fond of Dee, which is understandable as she is my sister. My feelings have been in turmoil for a while."

Beth paused and swallowed again. "But nothing I did worked. Dee could not be broken, and then Janet decided she wasn't going to taunt her any more. My plans were in tatters, and my mother's behaviour was getting more bizarre every day."

"So you killed Janet."

"No, but I think my mother did. She is very sick and not responsible for her actions."

Alan was beginning to believe her now, and upon reflection, what chance had Beth really had in life, being brought up by someone as twisted as Lizzie clearly was? Even now, she still had a loyalty to her mother. Her revelation that she was Dee's sister had been a huge surprise.

"Beth, I understand you have had a rocky life, but why didn't you take your mother to the doctor? From what you say, it sounds like she needs to be certified."

"I did take her, but she is crafty and can act normally when she has to. She was given anti-depressants, but they are no good to her. She drinks too much, and also takes drugs."

193

j

Alan could feel a wave of sympathy for this young girl. This case was so complicated. And her mother was on the loose, they had to find her.

"So you think your mother is capable of killing someone, then?"

"To be honest, I think she has lost it completely. She knew that Janet had refused to carry on taunting Dee, and next thing I know Janet is dead. She hates me spending any time with Dee. It started off as cover, so I could pretend to like her whilst working to rid us of her, but I have always felt a connection, and I really do love her."

"And Dee has no idea that you are related?"

"No, and I think my mother hates that we are related. That day when Janet refused to help any more, she got very angry, and she said she was going to finish them both. She was always saying stuff like that, but I made sure I went out with Dee to keep her safe."

"What did your mother do then?"

"Well, first off I put a sedative powder in her coffee, and I hoped she would sleep off her anger. I have used them before to defuse her. I knew she might wake up later, but then we saw Janet on her way to the beach, and I was pretty sure she was meeting Billy, she was very keen on him. My mother has taken to roaming around the beaches, sometimes on foot and sometimes on that motorbike. And then Dee said she was going to walk to Reculver via the beach, and I had to stop her, so I gave her a sedative powder in a can of Sprite, but it didn't seem to be working. She walked to the bus stop with me, and then I had to go through the charade of getting on the bus, and then off at the next stop, and hot footing it home to see if my mother was there. She arrived home after me, but has never admitted if she did kill Janet."

"And you say you don't know where your mother is now."

"She may be home. I can try her mobile, if she answers it."

"Good idea, then we can get her in for questioning, too."

Lizzie could hear bells ringing, and she thought she was at the church with Danny. They were getting louder and louder. They filled her head, and it felt like it would explode. She woke up with a bump, sweat was pouring off her, and her head was swirling.

Danny wasn't there after all, and she felt the pain of his loss again. Damn that drink. Her brain felt all fogged up, and she didn't know where she was.

She sat up in bed, and noticed her mobile was pulsing. She picked it up, and Beth's name flashed up.

"Mum, are you at home? I am at the police station, and they want to talk to you."

The fog started to clear from Lizzie's mind. She wasn't going to the police station. Nothing was going to stop her from getting her revenge! Damn those police. They were not coming to get her, and she was not going there, either, tonight.

"I am not at home. I went to Margate."

"Oh Mum, you're not on the beach again surely? You know you shouldn't use the car, it's not safe."

"I'll be back later," she said, and quickly put the phone down.

Beth was about to ask her to come back now, but the line went dead. Did she have Dee with her? Who knew?

"She said she was at Margate, and I didn't get a chance to ask about Dee. But it might not be true."

Alan sighed, this woman was difficult to pin down. But they best check out her house. "OK, we'll run you home and see if she's there. In the meantime, what is the registration of her car? We'll get the roads checked."

When Dee woke up it was dark. She was lying on a hard floor with her hands tied, as though she was praying. She was also blindfolded, but that didn't stop the strong musty smell from pervading her senses. She had been kidnapped and attacked by the same maniac all dressed in black that had tried to run her down in the glen.

But they were not going to get away with it! She had no idea where she was, but she did realise that this maniac wanted her dead, and she wasn't prepared to give up easily. It was completely quiet around her now, meaning they must have gone for now, so it was time to act, as they could come back any time soon.

All she remembered was being seized by someone dressed in a black leather outfit. But it wasn't a man, it was a woman with blonde hair, and a very angry face. Dee's face was throbbing with pain from where she had been hit.

She tried to twist her hands, but they were bound very tightly, and she could feel the cord digging into her skin. She wished she could sit up and take stock of the situation. She tried rocking sideways, but then fell onto her right side; that didn't help at all.

Next Dee rocked herself back to an upright position, and then pushed backwards. There seemed to be a wall behind her, but it wasn't brick, it felt light, so she guessed she might be in an old caravan. That would account for the musty smell.

She tried sucking on the blindfold which covered her whole face. It was thin material and flimsy, so she tried to bite it, and succeeded in making a tear. It felt like a silk scarf. Now she used her front teeth to work on it. She didn't have much saliva to help her because her throat was dry, and she hadn't had a drink for hours, but she just kept sucking. In the end it became limp, and then she managed to free her mouth.

But it still covered her eyes, and she couldn't use her hands. She could feel panic rushing through her, but she told herself very sternly that her life was at stake and she must keep control.

She took a deep breath and screamed as loud as she could. "Somebody please hep me!" And her voice echoed around her. She felt despair enveloping her. She must be in the middle of nowhere, and no one could hear her.

Using her elbows, she shuffled along the wall, and at the end it felt like a wooden shelf. It had a sharp edge, so she worked the cord that tied her hands against it. It seemed to her like hours, but probably was only minutes, before it finally frayed away and her hands were free.

She then removed the gag from her eyes, and rubbed her hands together to get the blood circulating again. She straightened up. Her eyes were getting used to the gloom and she could see the caravan door in front of her .

Dee opened it, but there was nothing but inky blackness outside, with what might be an outline of trees with branches blowing in the breeze. She had no idea where she was. In which direction should she run? But soon her mind was made up for her. She saw the lights of a car as it turned into the clearing where she was.

Instinct told her it was her captor. The headlights were full on, blinding her, and to her horror the car accelerated at speed towards her. She jumped as it reached her; she didn't want to die, and it just missed her.

Lizzie realised when she came off the phone, that the scumbag police could spoil all her plans, and she was not about to let that happen. If they brought Beth back, and then took her in, the bitch would not die. There would be no retribution.

Even if she pretended to be asleep tonight, in the morning Beth would want her to go to the police station, so it looked like she must do it now. Hopefully the bitch was as scared as hell of her. She would go back to the caravan and get rid of her. In Lizzie's muddled and confused mind, it did not occur to her that a blazing caravan would be a big giveaway. Nor did she really care what happened to her afterwards, as long as she could kill the bitch.

She didn't bother to dress. Something told her she had to get this job done quickly, so she jumped in the car still wearing her pyjamas. It shuddered into gear and moved forward. The caravan wasn't far away, and she had remembered to put a can of petrol in the back, which she had found in the shed.

The car was up to speed now, and as she rounded the corner by the clearing, she was enraged to see the bitch; she had escaped! How the hell had she managed that? She put her headlights on full beam, luckily they still worked, and drove straight towards Dee. But the stupid bitch had jumped out of the way.

She was determined to get it right this time, so she backed the car up ready to accelerate again. She saw the look of horror on Dee's face; she was trapped and, with a gleeful laugh, Lizzie drove straight at her.

Alan had decided to take Beth home. He was very curious to see her mother. If she really was out of her mind, they needed to bring her in. Locking Beth up overnight wouldn't achieve anything. If what she said was true, Beth had not had a normal life, and he was going to recommend that the council needed to find somewhere habitable for her to live.

As they reached the lane that led down to Reculver, Beth shouted.

"Look! There's my mother's car, turning into that clearing."

Alan skidded to a halt, and Beth was the first one to spring out. She saw the figure of Dee caught in her mother's headlights, and she froze with horror when she saw the car weaving its way towards her. Then her mother reversed, and when she realised she was going to try and run Dee down again, she screamed at her to stop. But Lizzie was not to be thwarted, and as she accelerated across the clearing, Beth could see that Dee was cornered, she had nowhere to go.

Without even thinking about it, Beth jumped in front of Dee, using her own body as a human shield. The car hit Beth full on, her body was flung into the air and then it landed with a sickening thud on the unforgiving concrete. Her arms and legs were splayed out at all angles, and there was blood dripping from her mouth. She looked just like a rag doll.

When Dee saw what had happened, her fear turned to anguish. There was her best friend laying there in a bad way, and she owed her life to her! She knelt down beside the still body and wept. Had she just lost the best friend she ever had?

Chapter Twenty-four

After the events of the previous night, Alan felt he must go round and speak to Dee. Her family were so relieved to have her safely back home, but there were a few things that Alan now needed to explain. In her own home, with her family around her, was the best place.

Lydia let them in and took them through to the conservatory, where Dee was sitting pale-faced, with Nathan doing his best to comfort her.

"Good afternoon, Dee. How are you today?" asked Alan kindly.

"OK," whispered Dee.

"She is very upset about Beth; not knowing if she will make it," explained Nathan.

Wendy spoke gently, "We hope she will. In the meantime we need to explain a lot to you."

Lydia went off to make some tea, and they all sat down. Alan noticed how caring Nathan was towards Dee. Blood relative or not, he was a loving father in every way.

Once the tea was poured, Alan came straight to the point.

"Firstly, Dee, we have to tell you that Beth is your half-sister, you share the same blood father."

Dee gave a gasp. Maybe this was why she had always felt so close to Beth.

"Of course, we don't have any DNA tests to prove it, but Danny Foster had an affair with Lizzie first, and Beth was born. Danny allegedly promised Lizzie a future, so when your mother became pregnant with you, and then Danny died, Lizzie blamed your mother for robbing her of a future with Danny. When they moved to Herne Bay, and realised your family lived here, and you were, in fact, in Beth's class, then Beth's mother lost it completely."

"Wow!" said Dee, still trying to get her head round the fact that Beth was her half-sister.

Alan continued. "Beth took control of the situation by becoming 'the boss', and manipulating Janet, so she was not innocent in all this. But we believe she was trying to make you leave the school, and possibly the neighbourhood as well, because of the way it was affecting her mother. She did not intend you to die, and the day her mother lost control and threatened to kill both you and Janet, she went to the cinema with you to keep you safe. She even put a powder in your can of Sprite, so you would go home, and not go to the beach alone."

"I thought it was fear of the Headland that made me faint."

"No, she admitted drugging you, but said you seemed OK when she got on the bus. She believed that Janet was with Billy and would be safe, so she then got off the bus and ran home to see what her mother was doing."

"Do you know for sure that her mother killed Janet?"

"Yes, we found some DNA on the back of Janet's head which matched Lizzie's. We also found the motorbike at the cottage. Beth, of course, no longer lives at Riverside Walk, but she kept that a secret. And as for you, we saw with our own eyes how Lizzie tried to kill you."

Dee was finding the whole story quite horrifying, but try as she might, she couldn't blame Beth for her part in it. With a crazy mother to cope with, Beth had done what she thought was best. Dee found herself also pitying Lizzie.

"What will happen to Beth's mother?"

"Well, she will never stand trial. She is not fit mentally to do so."

"So, if Beth does recover, she will be homeless without any family. Oh, it's awful!" said Dee, her eyes filling with tears.

Nathan wrapped his arms around her. "Dee, you worry too much about other people. What about yourself? Beth did some bad things to you."

"Yes she did, but she had her reasons, and I forgive her and just want her to recover," said Dee.

He had guessed she would say that. Dee had the kindest heart in the world. This is why she could never have killed anyone. And Nathan did understand what she meant, even he pitied Beth for the life she had endured with Lizzie.

"If Beth has no one, we will give her a home here, don't worry," he said, knowing it would cheer Dee a little.

Alan drained his cup and turned towards Wendy. She nodded in response.

"It's time we were going, but I hope this explains things more clearly to you."

"Yes, thank you, I will see you out," said Nathan.

As they drove back towards Whitstable, they were realising their job was nearly over. Wendy didn't mind, as she was feeling a bit homesick, but Alan's mind was going over all the advantages of living in this area. He spoke his thoughts out loud.

"It's been an interesting four weeks, and you have been your usual loyal self, Wendy, especially when I had to call you out at dinnertime yesterday evening, but it got the job done."

"Yes sir. It's sad for Beth that she has such a mentally sick mother."

"Indeed, after seeing her this morning, the doctor says he believes that Lizzie was suffering from untreated postnatal depression, and then had a mental breakdown about a year ago, coupled with other mental problems. The only pills she was taking were anti-depressants, which were clearly not enough. I think she may well need to be detained for the rest of her life."

"Yes," said Wendy, "and the irony of the situation is that Dee was bullied because her own mother had mental problems, and yet Beth's mother was far worse."

"Yes, talk about the pot calling the kettle black," laughed Alan. "You can now enjoy the rest of Sunday, and tomorrow we will present ourselves for the last time."

He watched as Wendy walked into the hotel entrance. He had Sunday afternoon off, so he could go back and spend it with his family. He had enjoyed being here for the last four weeks, and it had

201

certainly been great for Zoe to have the support of her family whilst Adam was so young, but when they got home that would all stop, and he would be back to working crazy hours.

Later, when he told Zoe they would be leaving the next day, he saw the disappointment in her eyes. She loved it here too. "Don't worry, we will visit," he said encouragingly.

In bed that night, Zoe shared her thoughts with him. "I would love to bring Adam up here in the lovely clean air. London is getting more and more polluted. Is there any possibility you could get a transfer?"

"But what about your job? I thought that when the year is up, you would want to go back to the hospital."

"I thought I did. But since I have become a mum, it's the best thing in the world. Maybe we should try for baby number two when Adam is a bit older. The thing with nursing is I can go back any time, and it would be part time, my family would always come first."

Alan kissed her on the brow. "In that case I will certainly enquire, even if it means going on a transfer list."

Zoe hugged him tightly. "Now I know why I love you." Then she turned over and went peacefully off to sleep.

The next morning Alan and Wendy arrived at Canterbury Police Station at nine o'clock. As they entered the room where the team were all gathered, they were greeted by clapping, which was led by Gary.

"Well done to you both!" said Gary

"Thanks, we got there eventually, and now it's time to head back to Wimbledon," said Alan, with a grimace.

"You mean you don't want to?" said Gary, looking amazed.

"Let's just say this area has grown on me. Fresh air, beaches and countryside, what's not to like?"

"You could always apply for a transfer. I reckon, after solving this case, Kevin Watts would help you with anything."

"I am going to put in for a transfer. Sometimes they take years, but I am going to try," said Alan.

They had both packed, and expected to travel back after lunch. He knew that Zoe was going to miss her parents, but they had promised to return soon for a holiday. In the meantime Alan picked up the necessary forms to fill out for a transfer. As they left the police station, Wendy spoke.

"Can we go to the hospital? It's only up the road from here. Just to see how Beth is doing before we go?"

Alan's face looked sad. "Of course, I was thinking of that, too."

He drove to the hospital, and after inquiring where Beth was, they found themselves outside the room where she lay. As they were not relatives, but were police, this was as far as they were allowed to go. They were only allowed to view her through the window, and when Alan saw the still slight figure laying there, with machines working to keep her alive and tubes everywhere, it didn't look good.

Alan spoke to her doctor, who explained that Beth had suffered internal injuries as well as hitting her head. He said, although they were doing everything they could to keep her alive, the prognosis was not good. They left the hospital in very sober spirits, and Alan felt grateful that he had the love of his wife and son. This poor young girl had nothing.

Chapter Twenty-five

The newspapers were once again full of the story of the girl who was murdered on the beach, but this time they had a new slant on it. There had been a mad woman dressed in black who carried out many evil deeds, and it certainly made interesting reading.

Beth was only mentioned at the end of the story, as she had been run over by her own mother who had been trying to kill her best friend. But Beth had become a heroine for shielding Dee from her own mother, and now she was in hospital fighting for her life, so she might never know how much accolade she had received both online and in the press.

After reading the stories, and seeing the photographs, it didn't take Brian and Molly Harper long to realise that the culprit was their estranged daughter Lizzie, and her very ill daughter was their granddaughter. They were now filled with guilt for abandoning Lizzie when she had most needed them, and they continually wished they could turn the clock back and act differently.

The press reported that Lizzie had been sectioned and was unlikely ever to be fit enough to stand trial. Her daughter Beth was in a Canterbury Hospital, but there was very little hope that she would survive, and even if she did she might have brain damage.

Molly was all for dropping everything, and journeying from London to Canterbury, but Brian was more cautious, telling her to wait and see if Beth pulled through. He felt if they went dashing down there, and Beth didn't make it, the press would have a field day and add even more drama to the story. He could just see the headlines: DESPERATE ESTRANGED GRANDPARENTS TOO LATE TO SEE THEIR GRANDDAUGHTER. They both felt bad enough for never getting to know Beth, and this would only hammer it home more. So they kept in contact with the hospital to try and find out about her progress.

Beth was in a coma for a month, and during that time Dee came every day to see her, and sat holding her hand and trying to will her to live. The staff had encouraged her to do that. Anything to try and stimulate Beth's brain back into life.

Then Beth woke up and started to speak, just a little, but she kept falling asleep again. And still Dee sat holding her hand, and talking slowly and gently to her. The doctors warned Dee that it would be a long process; Beth might never walk again and her brain might be damaged. But nothing deterred Dee, she still went to see Beth every day.

Molly and Brian were told they could come and visit Beth now she was awake, but not to expect too much too soon. When they came into her room, her long blonde hair framed the pillow and her innocent blue eyes studied them with surprise. She had no idea who they were.

She reminded them so much of Lizzie when she was a girl. Molly gently explained who they were, and how they wanted to see her get better. At first she was a bit wary of them, but gradually they started to win her confidence. Living in London, and working up there too, meant they could not come every day, but they came regularly twice a week.

Dee was so pleased that Beth did have some family. She became friendly with them, too, and they watched Beth getting stronger every day. One morning Beth asked Dee where her mother was, and with her heart aching for her, she told her she was having medical care because of her mental condition. Beth did shed some tears, and Dee understood why. In spite of everything that had happened, Beth would always love the only mother she had ever known.

After three months, Beth was helped out of bed to sit on a chair. She had lost weight, and her limbs were wasted, so the physiotherapist set to work on her legs, rubbing them, and eventually encouraging her to bear her own weight, and then try to walk a few steps.

The hospital felt she could now go home, and attend the hospital regularly for further physiotherapy, but Beth didn't have a home. It was unthinkable that she could return to the damp and musty cottage. Knowing how happy it would make Dee, Nathan and Lydia offered her a place with them. They also invited Molly and Brian to carry on visiting her at their house, knowing how important it was to keep the family bonds.

Brian and Molly very much wanted to give Beth a home with them. They were both in their middle fifties and worked in London, which was where their home was. They could see how close to Dee Beth was, just like sisters would be, and they were not sure she could cope with leaving Dee. They even discussed it with Nathan and Lydia, who understood their fears. Nathan's advice was to simply try asking Beth.

So six months after the fateful day when she had almost lost her life, Brian and Molly offered Beth a home with them, and an opportunity to attend sixth form college in London. For the very first time Beth spoke about her mother to them.

"I am very sad that my mum is so sick in her mind, and I promise you I won't make the mistakes she did. I will work hard and get a good career. If I make any mistakes in my life, I will never blame anyone else. Somebody once said to me, we make our own happiness, and I know exactly what he meant."

"You are so right," said Molly, with feeling.

Beth smiled at her grandparents. For the first time in her life she felt wanted and loved, but her smile was tinged with sadness. "I am so grateful to you for offering me a home, but one thing I can't do is cut myself off from Dee. She means everything to me."

Molly was touched by her sincerity. These two girls had a bond that would remain constant in spite of everything that had happened. They could not save Lizzie from herself, but, as grandparents, they had a second chance with Beth.

"Don't worry, you will still be able to see Dee. She can come and stay with us sometimes. You are sisters, and there will be many opportunities to get together."

Dee had known that one day Beth might leave Herne Bay, and she knew she mustn't be selfish, so when Beth told her she was moving to London, she hugged her warmly. The main thing was she had survived, and she did have a family who cared about her.

"Beth, I owe my life to you. That was such a brave thing you did to save me!" she said, remembering that terrifying feeling when she saw Lizzie driving so madly towards her.

Beth blushed, she didn't feel as if she deserved any praise, because her actions had been the cause of her mother's bid to kill Dee. With a wisdom which not many seventeen year olds would possess, she now realised that instead of doing what her mother wanted and trying to rid herself of Dee, she should have put her foot down, and made sure her sick mother had the mental treatment that she needed. It was a big lesson in life to learn at such a young age, and she would always be sad that her mother had been unable to stop herself from ruining her own life. All the attention that she was getting as a local heroine, she did not feel she had earned.

"Dee, when we are talking about saving lives, the doctor told me that you never left my bedside when it looked like all hope was gone, and you willed me back to life. So I think I should be the one to do the thanking."

They both embraced warmly, and not until after she had gone did Dee give way to her emotions and shed some tears. Nathan was there to comfort her. "Daddy, I will miss her," she sobbed.

"Of course you will, but be proud of how well she is doing now. All your support got her out of that coma, you gave her back her life."

"Do you think so?" said Dee, wonderingly. To her it had felt like the right thing to do, to try and help her, especially after she had risked her own life to save Dee.

"I certainly do. The doctors all said it's a miracle that she survived, and without a mother to guide her, life has been really tough for her. But now she can put down roots with her grandparents. They are nice people, and we can all keep in touch."

"She has another chance now, I suppose."

"She certainly does, and so do you. Now you can concentrate on your exams, and it will be much easier when you retake them. There won't be any more bullying, and don't forget about Jenny, she is a good friend."

"Now, Daddy, I am not a gooseberry. Jenny and Jack are an item now."

They both laughed at that. Gawky, but likable, Jack, had now forsaken his bike and his computer for long walks with Jenny and Rex. Jenny had finally realised how much he liked her.

Something now struck Dee. "I can relaunch my Facebook page again. It's time I was back on social media."

Nathan smiled. He was so very proud of his girl. She was such a star!